WIFE
FOR HIRE

JEAN KARR 4/01 10.00

WIFE
FOR HIRE

•

Marilyn Shank

AVALON BOOKS
NEW YORK

This book is dedicated to my grandchildren:
ASHLEY, KELSEY, TYLER and ADAM

Chapter One

The taxi sped down the dirt road, spitting dust clouds into the bright afternoon sunshine. When it stopped in front of a sprawling ranch house surrounded by majestic mountains, Gabriella Gibson caught her breath. Never in her wildest dreams had she imagined she'd end up on a cattle ranch.

She paid the driver, grabbed her suitcases and climbed out. Gathering every ounce of her flagging courage, she walked toward the ranch house and rapped on the door.

A short, round-faced cowboy with carrot-red hair and a beard answered. Was he Clayborne Forrester?

"Afternoon, ma'am," he said. "Can I help you?"

"Well, um, yes. Clayborne is expecting me," she stammered, not knowing where to begin.

"Come in. May I tell the boss who's calling?"

Relief flooded Gaby as she realized this man wasn't

Mr. Forrester. "Tell him . . ." She paused, finding it difficult to actually mouth the words. "Tell him his wife has arrived."

The man's blue eyes widened. "That's impossible. You see, Mr. Forrester's a bachelor."

"Not anymore. Clayborne and I got married last night. In Colorado Springs." Her voice trembled as she put the staggering lie into words.

The man ran a hand across his neatly trimmed beard. "Married? Well, I'll be danged. Hang on a minute. I'll tell the boss you're here."

As the cowboy moved toward a massive oak staircase, Gaby considered bolting for the door. When she'd answered the ad in a theater journal, promising big bucks for a few weeks of playacting, it sounded like the answer to her problems. Now, she wasn't so sure.

Moments later, heavy footsteps descended the stairs. Gaby glanced up as two scuffed leather boots came into view. Next a pair of denim jeans emerged, secured at the waist by an antique-silver belt buckle. Then a turquoise cotton shirt with rolled-up sleeves that exposed tanned, muscular forearms. Finally, a handsome, angular face appeared, topped by a head of jet-black hair. It was like the methodical unveiling of a Remington painting.

Until this moment, the only cowboys Gaby had ever seen came in the form of movie stars. Looking at this flesh-and-blood model caused her to draw a shaky breath.

Turning to face the stranger who was her "husband," Gaby said, "Clayborne, darling," nearly choking on the words.

The great-looking man strode forward and pulled her into his arms where she was suddenly surrounded by the aroma of leather and fresh-scented aftershave. "Gabriella, sweetheart." Then he bent to kiss her.

As the cowboy's lips met hers, Gaby's pulse rate skittered into the danger zone. She'd never dreamed the man would kiss her within thirty seconds of her arrival! While she wanted to cry out in protest, she was supposed to be his wife. The greeting wasn't inappropriate.

When the mind-numbing kiss ended, Gaby's pretend husband wrapped an arm around her waist. "Jonas," Mr. Forrester said, "this is Gabriella, my bride. Honey, meet Jonas Miller, my foreman."

The foreman grinned. "Welcome to the Silver Saddle Ranch, Miz Forrester."

Gaby fought to regain control of both her voice and her breath. "Nice to meet you, Mr. Miller."

"Jonas will do. We're pretty informal around here. Shall I take the bags upstairs?"

Mr. Forrester nodded. "That will be fine, Jonas. I'll be up shortly, and we'll hammer out that budget."

The foreman grinned. "No hurry, boss. Looks like you've got more important things to do."

A flush warmed Gaby's cheeks. When the foreman was out of earshot, she whirled to face her counterfeit husband. "How dare you kiss me like that!"

Mr. Forrester frowned. "What did you expect from your new bridegroom? A handshake? Convincing my staff we're married is the first step in our little drama."

Gaby tried to tamp down her emotions. "Well, in the future, don't kiss me unless it's absolutely necessary."

The cowboy eyed her soberly. "Listen, Miss Gibson, it's in both our best interests for this 'marriage' to succeed."

"Then you'd better stop calling me Miss Gibson. Your staff is bound to suspect."

A grin teased the corners of the cowboy's appealing mouth. "I suppose first names are in order. Do you prefer Gaby or Gabriella?"

"Either is fine. What about you? Clayborne or Clay?"

He shrugged those incredibly broad shoulders. "The only person who gets away with Clayborne is my mother."

"Clay, then," she said, trying his name on for size.

"We have lots to learn about each other. Have you ever lived on a ranch?"

"Never."

"Ever visited one?"

"No."

"Do you read westerns?"

"Rarely. I picked one up at the airport but I've only read the first chapter."

He sighed. "In other words, you're completely unfamiliar with ranch life."

"I learn fast," she said, not wanting him to fire her within minutes of her arrival.

His gaze took Gaby in from head to toe, making her pulse skitter. "Are all your clothes so . . ." He paused as if he couldn't find the proper adjective to describe her clothing.

She planted her hands on her hips. "What, exactly, is wrong with this dress?"

"Nothing, if you were having lunch in the city. But ranchers' wives rarely wear dresses. I hope you brought jeans. And a pair of boots."

"Of course, I brought jeans. But I don't own any boots."

He sighed. "We'll manage. I'll take you upstairs so you can unpack."

At that moment, a large, incredibly shaggy dog bounded into the living room. A regular dust mop on steroids. The animal lunged at Gaby, settled its huge paws on her chest, and licked her cheek. Its tongue felt like an industrial-strength sponge.

Clay grasped the dog's collar and yanked him down. "Behave yourself, Jackson. That's no way to greet a lady."

The dog plopped into a heap beside the sofa. His tail beat rhythmically on the hardwood floor as he gazed at Gaby with soulful eyes.

"Uh, oh. I'm afraid Jackson left his signature." Clay pointed to a pair of muddy footprints on the bodice of her dress, symmetrically planted above each of her breasts.

She took a steadying breath. "Don't worry. This dress is washable. What kind of dog is it?" she asked, praying the enormous creature stay where he was.

"An Old English Sheepdog."

Suddenly Gaby sneezed—a violent allergy sneeze that shook her entire frame. Then she sneezed again. And again. The dog sprang to his feet and started barking. He sounded like a low-pitched foghorn.

When her sneezing subsided, she fished a tissue from

her pocket. "Excuse me, but I'm allergic to dust and animal dander. Is your dog always so . . . so friendly?"

"Not many women visit the ranch and Jackson's always been a lady's man. Are you ready to go upstairs?"

"I suppose so."

It wasn't true. She'd rather stay here and fight it out with Jackson than follow this great-looking cowboy upstairs.

But she had no choice. As she followed Clayborne Forrester to the second floor, she realized what a powerful man he was. The jeans he wore outlined solid, muscular legs, and his cotton shirt defined his wide shoulders and biceps. The man was a powerhouse. He looked like he could rope steers blindfolded.

Gaby entered the master bedroom wishing she hadn't gotten herself into this predicament. But she'd promised Mama she'd pay off the medical bills. If that meant becoming the pretend bride of this rugged cowboy, so be it.

Glancing out the window, Gaby saw a breathtaking view of the Rockies. The snowcapped mountain peaks stood in bold relief against a cornflower-blue sky. "How gorgeous," she murmured.

Clay's expression softened. "You can't beat the scenery in Colorado. I'd never live anywhere else."

Gaby reluctantly pulled her attention back to the room, which was furnished with country oak furniture. A plaid couch that had seen better days nestled beneath the eaves. A large oil painting above the bed portrayed a cattle drive so realistically you could almost hear the animals' hooves hitting the ground.

Clay cleared his throat. "This is . . . um . . . our bedroom."

"What do you mean, *our* bedroom? Don't you have a guest room?"

He crossed his arms over that broad chest. "My ranch hands are in and out all day. They'd think it was mighty strange for my bride to sleep across the hall."

She sighed, knowing he was right, but wondering how she could possibly share a room with this gorgeous man.

"Trust me, Gabriella, you have nothing to fear. I'll sleep on the couch and you can have my bed."

Gaby could swear he was glowering at her. She glowered right back. "I don't expect you to give up your bed. You work hard and need your rest. So I'll sleep on the couch."

"You'll be working pretty hard yourself." After a pause, he added, "I reckon we could take turns."

"Fair enough."

"By the way, can you cook?"

She stuck out her chin, not wanting to admit her culinary skills were limited. "Of course, I can cook."

"Then you can take over for Randy. You'll get the hang of how the ranch operates before my parents arrive."

Gaby tried to suppress her mounting panic. "Your parents? When we talked on the phone, you didn't say anything about your parents."

"My father's seriously ill. Dad's always wanted me to be as happily married as he and Mom are. The pretend marriage is to make Dad's last days happier."

"I see," she said, glad he cared about his family. "How long will they stay?"

"Less than a week."

Clay ran a hand over his forehead, bringing Gaby's attention back to his ruggedly handsome features. Dark brows and lashes framed his magnificent eyes and his cheeks held a hint of dimples.

He eyed her skeptically. "We only have a few days to convince Mom and Dad that we're head over heels in love, and that our marriage will last a lifetime, like theirs has."

Suddenly the assignment sounded overwhelming. "Is that all? Couldn't we build a barn some afternoon? Or fence in the entire acreage?"

His gray eyes narrowed. "I explained on the phone that this was a tough assignment. That's why I'm paying top dollar. If you don't want the job, say so. I'll put you on the next plane to Atlanta."

While Clay's suggestion sounded tempting, Gaby remembered the medical bills towering on her desk back home. Paying them off on her teacher's salary was impossible.

"I'm not backing out," she affirmed. "I fully intend to go through with this marriage."

Clay nodded. "That's more like it. Do you have any questions?"

Gaby's mind reeled with questions that she knew must be worked out as they went along. "Not at the moment."

"We'll inch our way through this," Clay said. "Do you want to freshen up after your long trip?"

"Yes, thanks."

Even more than a shower, Gaby wanted to escape this breathtaking cowboy. While he wasn't the kind of man she wanted to marry, he made her emotions stand up and take notice. As he stood there, in all his masculine glory, she wondered how she'd ever survive even a pretend marriage to him.

"I told Randy we'd have a guest for supper. I'll . . ." Clay paused and Gaby saw a flush of color creep up his neck. "I'll announce our marriage then."

She exhaled slowly. "Fine."

Her new bridegroom finally strode out of the bedroom and closed the door. Gaby dropped onto the couch, realizing she was in big trouble. She'd thought this job would be a snap. Normally, she could act her way through anything. But she hadn't factored in a runaway attraction to her pretend husband.

A lot of her college friends had dreamed of lassoing themselves a cowboy. But that wasn't Gaby's fantasy. She wanted a man from the South. A business man who dressed in tailored suits. Someone she could attend plays with and explore all the cultural activities Atlanta had to offer. Someone very different from this rough-looking cowboy.

Gaby felt shaken by her first encounter with Clayborne Forrester. It seemed her emotions had taken her brain captive. *It's a job, nothing more*, she reminded herself sternly, determined not to let her emotions take charge.

You're out of your mind, Clay told himself as he strode down the hall to his office. He dropped into his chair and buried his face in his hands. What ridiculous steps he was taking to fulfill his father's fondest wish.

His dad's recent heart attack and the doctor's dire prognosis shook Clay to his very core. He wanted desperately to brighten his father's last days and only one thing could accomplish that: if Clay were happily married.

But when he'd come downstairs to greet his pretend bride, he'd gotten the shock of his life. Gabriella Gibson looked more like a fashion model than a rancher's wife. Her eyes were green as a mountain stream, and she wore her thick blonde hair pinned back into a bun. Instead of dressing for the part, the woman had shown up in a pink dress with a scooped neck and high-heeled pumps. He tried to forget that his heart took a nose-dive the moment he laid eyes on her.

High-heeled pumps have no function on a cattle ranch, he reminded himself. And neither did Gabriella Gibson.

To make matters worse, the lady was allergic to dust and animal hair. Why, a cattle ranch was made up almost entirely of dust and animal hair! How would he ever pass off this classy-looking, allergic woman as his wife?

Jonas stepped into the office and cut Clay's ruminations short. "So you went and got yourself married. And didn't invite me to the wedding!"

Clay raked a hand through his hair and forced a smile. "It all happened pretty fast. You know, love at first sight."

"Well, you picked yourself a real beauty. But then

you've always had great taste in women. Guess I'm surprised you married again—after Jill, and all."

The reminder of his disastrous marriage to Jill brought a wave of sad memories. Clay had believed Jill was the love of his life. That their marriage would last forever. Unfortunately, Jill hadn't seen it that way.

"I didn't plan to marry again. It just sort of happened."

His foreman grinned. "They say love sneaks up on a man."

"Listen, Jonas, I'd rather you didn't mention my . . . ah . . . marriage to the hands just yet. I'll announce it at supper."

Jonas shrugged. "You're the boss."

Clay sighed, wondering how he would convince anyone Gabriella was his wife when he couldn't say the word marriage without stumbling all over it.

Anxious to get his mind back on work and off his new bride, he said, "Let's tackle that budget now."

As Clay opened the appropriate file on his computer, he realized that, like it or not, the pretense had begun. He only hoped he and the gorgeous Miss Gibson from Atlanta could make this marriage seem real.

For his father's sake.

Gaby opened Clay's closet and found it crammed with cowboy clothes. Stiff denim jeans mingled with dark corduroy shirts and an assortment of fringed jackets and vests. His clothes smelled of leather and the fresh, earthy scent Gaby nearly drowned in when Clay kissed her. Just thinking of that kiss sent excitement swirling through her body.

She reached for some spare hangers and, with trembling fingers, hung her things alongside his. Her pastel clothes looked out of place beside the dark garments. Like spring flowers drowning in a thunderstorm.

After unpacking, Gaby placed a gilt-framed photograph of Mama on the oak dresser. She smiled, glad she'd finally be able to keep her promise to Mama.

She caught her reflection in the mirror and sighed. Her mascara had streaked and she'd nervously chewed off every trace of lipstick. Jackson's paw prints still loomed above her breasts. She couldn't meet Clay's cowboys looking like the victim of a wild animal attack.

After gathering her toiletries, Gaby headed for the bathroom, which contained a claw-foot tub circled by a plastic shower curtain. She'd need to soak in this tub often to survive her "marriage" to this rugged cowboy. But for now, she'd grab a quick shower, wash her hair, and dress for dinner.

Gaby pulled a navy-blue bath towel from a rattan shelf in the corner, slipped out of her clothes, and turned on the spray. As the peppering of the warm water caressed her skin, some of the pent-up anxiety slipped away, making her feel more confident. She could, and would, keep the emotion out of this relationship. After all, she was an actress, wasn't she?

After showering, Gaby wrapped the fluffy towel around herself, hurried back to the bedroom, and locked the door. She'd just finished blow-drying her hair when a knock sounded. "Gabriella, let me in."

A sense of panic whirled through her. There was no way Clay Forrester was coming into her bedroom. Well, his actually. "You'll have to come back later," she said firmly.

"I can't. Now, let me in."

Gaby flipped back the lock and cracked the door slightly. "Wait till I finish dressing." She started closing the door again but Clay stuck a scuffed cowboy boot in the doorway, making that impossible.

"Jonas walked by a moment ago," he whispered. "What will he think if you bar me from my own bedroom?"

"Give me five minutes," she pleaded.

"Then at least hand me some clothes," Clay said, describing the ones he wanted.

She sighed. "All right. Wait right here."

Gaby went to his closet and located the clothing he'd asked for. When she handed it to him, he said, "I'll pick you up in half an hour. If that suits you."

She nodded. "That suits me just fine."

With great relief, Gaby closed the door behind Clay and locked it again.

For the first time ever, she questioned her acting skills. Could she play the part of loyal wife to this powerful man without being carried away by her feelings of attraction?

She'd laughed at Susan, her college roommate, who'd dreamed of marrying a cowboy and eventually did. Now that dream didn't seem quite so absurd.

Gaby sighed. If only Clayborne Forrester had been an average-looking man like his foreman. Then she could have pulled this charade off without a hitch.

As she dressed for dinner, Gaby again reminded her-

self why she'd come to this ranch in the middle of nowhere. Mama had been devastated when she couldn't
pay her medical bills. And because Gaby couldn't bear
the pain in Mama's eyes, she'd told her to stop worrying,
that she'd pay every last cent. Mama died peacefully,
taking comfort in Gaby's promise.

But how would Mama feel if she knew her daughter
had ended up in Land's End, Colorado, a tiny town just
west of Denver? Would she disapprove of her pretend
marriage to this drop-dead gorgeous cowboy?

Gaby couldn't think about that right now. Pushing her
anxiety aside, she applied fresh makeup and styled her
hair. She wanted to look her best for her first meal as
Clayborne Forrester's bride.

Chapter Two

"**R**eady to go downstairs, Mrs. Forrester?"

Startled by Clay's deep voice, Gaby glanced up from the magazine she'd been scanning to find him waiting at the open bedroom door. She drew a tentative breath, stood, and walked toward him. "Ready as I'll ever be."

His gaze was bold and assessed her frankly. She glanced down at her cotton skirt and blouse, wondering if she'd dressed wrong again. "I hope this is appropriate for dinner."

"Supper. We call it supper around here."

"Supper, then." *Would she and this cowboy ever speak the same language?*

He nodded. "The outfit will do nicely."

As they walked toward the stairway, Gaby's nerves felt taut as a tightrope. "I know we rehearsed our story on the telephone. I just hope I can keep it all straight."

15

"If we listen to each other and don't supply more information than necessary, we'll keep our stories in sync."

Clay looked first-rate in his crisp white shirt, dark leather vest, and a pair of form-fitting denim jeans. The clean scent she'd nearly drowned in earlier again made her lightheaded. He gripped Gaby's elbow as they descended the stairs and his warm touch caused a flutter in the pit of her stomach.

As they passed through the dining room, the heavy aroma of grilling steaks greeted them. "I hope you'll be comfortable in my house," Clay stated.

"I'll manage just fine," she asserted. "After all, I'm here to work, not to enjoy myself."

His mouth curved into a wry smile. "Maybe we could manage to do both."

"Maybe," Gaby said, wondering what he meant by that.

A burst of laughter erupted from the kitchen, but when they entered the room, the laughter ceased. Chairs scraped back from the table as several cowboys sprang to their feet.

"Wow! You weren't kidding when you said we were having a guest for supper." That observation came from a young ranch hand who stood at the stove frying potatoes.

Clay turned to Gaby. "Randy's not too good with words. That's his way of saying he thinks you're pretty."

She felt herself blush. "Well, thanks for the compliment."

When Clay suddenly wrapped an arm around her waist and pulled her close, more heat rose in Gaby's cheeks.

She slipped her arm around his waist, trying to act like an excited new bride. And for a moment, she almost felt like one.

Her pretend husband cleared his throat. "Fellas, I'd like you to meet a special lady. This is Gabriella. Gaby, for short."

"Howdy, ma'am," came the cowboy chorus. Grins spread over the men's suntanned faces.

"Honey, let me introduce my ranch hands," Clay continued. "You've already met Randy and Jonas. These other characters are Zack Adams and his twin brother Zeb."

Callused hands shot out and shook Gaby's warmly. "Nice to have you visit," one of the Adams twins said. Gaby wasn't sure which one. They looked like a couple of cowboy bookends.

"She isn't visiting." Clay hesitated, obviously struggling to put their absurd situation into words. "Gabriella and I got married last night."

For a moment, the room grew silent. Then the same Adams brother reached out and smacked Clay on the back. "That's great, boss. All the best."

After hearty congratulations were offered, Clay cleared his throat. "We'd better eat these steaks while they're still hot." He ushered Gaby to a long trestle table edged by two wooden benches. They took one bench while the Adams brothers and Jonas took the other.

Randy placed a platter of sizzling steaks in the center of the table and added heaping bowls of fried potatoes, baked beans topped with bacon strips, and several loaves of French bread. Then he joined them.

Gaby cringed as she took a huge steak from the platter Jonas held for her. Since she rarely ate meat, this piece was a six-month supply.

"So where did you meet Miz Gaby?" Randy asked.

"In Atlanta," Clay replied. "Remember when I visited my sister last February? She introduced us."

"Annie's a good friend of mine," Gaby affirmed, hoping to keep pace with both their fabricated married life and the half a cow that covered her plate.

"Amy," Clay corrected. "My sister's name is Amy."

"I meant Amy. She and I met at . . ."

Suddenly, Gaby's mind went blank. She had no idea where she and Amy were supposed to have met.

Fortunately, Clay took over. "You exercise at the same health club."

Recognition flashed. "Yes, we do. At Gold's Gym. Amy's quite the fitness nut."

"Where did you get married?" asked the other Adams brother.

"In Colorado Springs," Gaby replied, glad she could answer one question right.

Randy looked puzzled. "If you got married last night, how come the boss came back to the ranch alone?"

Gaby took a steadying breath before launching in. "You see," she said, trying to explain, "my aunt lives in Colorado Springs and has been, um, quite ill. Aunt, um, Betsy begged me to come see her but I couldn't get away. So I spent last night with her, and took a taxi to the ranch this afternoon."

Randy looked as if he didn't follow the logistics and

Gaby couldn't blame him. She'd gotten lost, too. Some-where between Denver and Colorado Springs.

"Have you two seen each other lately? I don't remem-ber you leaving the ranch in the past three months, boss." The first Adams brother shot a gaping hole in their plot development.

Clay shifted uncomfortably. "Well, uh, no. We didn't exactly see each other."

"I teach drama in an Atlanta high school," Gaby in-terjected, "so I couldn't take time off while school was in session." She sighed. That was the first true statement she'd uttered all evening.

A drop of perspiration skittered down Clay's forehead and he swiped at it with the back of his hand. He sat so close to Gaby it made her nervous. The rancher's pow-erful presence wasn't helping her concentration any. Glancing at Jonas, an average-looking fellow, she again wished he'd been the owner of the Silver Saddle Ranch.

Since her "husband" wasn't adding to their story, Gaby figured it was her turn. "Clay and I planned to spend some time together when school let out for the summer. But one evening, while talking on the tele-phone, we decided to get married instead."

The cowboys looked baffled at first, but Gaby flashed her most dazzling smile and they smiled right back. While they seemed to accept this wedding without dif-ficulty, the thought of marrying the handsome man be-side her made Gaby's heart flutter wildly.

"Are you taking a honeymoon?" Randy inquired.

Clay wiped away another bead of perspiration. "Maybe later. When things slow down around here."

The ranch hands finally turned their attention to the business of eating. When they'd sat down, there'd been enough staples here to see Gaby through a hard winter. But within minutes, the platters and bowls were nearly empty.

"More potatoes, ma'am?" Jonas asked.

"No, thanks. I've had it."

She had, too. Both with this meal and the charade unfolding around her.

Randy shook his head. "It's not right, you two not going on a honeymoon."

Gaby covered her pretend husband's hand with her own. Just touching this man sent delicious shivers down her spine. "Clay and I are together," she said smiling sweetly into his fascinating eyes. "That's all that matters."

There. She ought to get an Emmy for that little performance.

"Gaby and I discussed what her responsibilities will be at the ranch," Clay said, changing the subject. "She'll do the cooking. Randy, that'll free you to help build the split rail fence."

"Great. I'd rather build fences than cook any day."

"Then it's settled. Gaby, why don't we do the dishes and let these fellas head for the bunkhouse?"

Randy shook his head. "No way. This is your weddin' night. Nobody washes dishes on their weddin' night. Now you two go take a walk or something. We'll clean this mess in no time."

Clay turned to her. "Want to take a walk, sweetheart?"

The rumble of her rancher-husband's deep voice and

the way it lingered on the word "sweetheart" made Gaby's senses spin. "I'd love a walk," she said softly.

Clay escorted her out the kitchen door and as they stepped into the balmy June evening, he extended his hand. "Normally, I wouldn't be so bold as to hold your hand, but we've got to keep up appearances."

She only hesitated a moment before sliding her hand into Clay's. When his fingers circled hers, a tingling sensation swirled through her body. She tried to throttle the dizzying current racing through her but it refused to go away.

As they headed for the open country, Gaby gave herself a mental shake. She reminded herself that holding this handsome rancher's hand was just a mechanical act to give credence to their little performance. But she couldn't deny it was a delightful mechanical act. One that made her feel vibrantly alive.

They walked along the split-rail fence that stretched on for miles. "You mean all this land is yours?" Gaby asked, thrilled both by the incredible countryside and the rugged rancher's nearness.

"As far as the eye can see."

"It must take forever to mow the grass."

Clay flashed that incredible grin. "Actually, the cattle do most of the mowing."

They passed the bunkhouse, several barns, and finally reached a stretch of open country where a herd of cows grazed. "What kind are they?"

"Black Angus. The Silver Saddle's known for our high-quality breed. We raise strong, healthy cattle."

Pride echoed in Clayborne Forrester's sensual voice.

And rightly so. All the land, as far as the eye could see, was his land. So was every single cow that stood grazing upon it.

Gaby felt like a trespasser. After all, she'd come here under false pretenses. *Does all nature know about our little charade*? she wondered.

The leaves seemed to whisper their secret and the red sun flashed a warning as it sank in the flaming sky. One of the cows let out a sustained moo, probably informing the rest of the herd about their preposterous hoax.

"We're well out of sight." Clay released her hand and Gaby immediately missed his touch. He quirked an eyebrow. "How'd you feel we handled the announcement of our marriage?"

"Not great. I couldn't remember your sister's name much less where she and I supposedly met."

Clay's eyes flashed mischievously. "As names go, Amy's pretty simple. Just three letters."

"Well, you didn't help by saying we hadn't *exactly* seen each other since February."

He shook his head. "This game of pretend is tougher than I imagined."

As they strolled on, Gaby said, "I've never lived with a bunch of cowboys and it's a bit unnerving. Are there other women around?"

"Of course. Adrienne Mason and her husband Jack own the Circle J. And Bonnie Masterson and her husband Kevin have the Lazy Diamond. Both ranches adjoin the Silver Saddle."

"Will I meet them? In Atlanta, I have lots of girlfriends. We play Bridge on Thursday evenings and my sorority meets twice a month."

"The neighbors have lots of get-togethers. The Masons are hosting a barn dance day after tomorrow."

Clay turned to face Gaby and when his gray eyes met hers, she again felt jolted by the electrical current sparking between them. She could drown in the dark intensity of this man's gaze.

"Would you like to go?" he asked.

"Go where?"

For the life of her, Gaby couldn't remember what they were talking about.

"To the barn dance."

"Oh, yes," she said, rejoining the conversation. "I'd love to."

"Then it's settled."

Gaby felt thankful when they started walking again. She could hold onto her train of thought as she gazed at the fantastic countryside. Not so while looking into Clay's mesmerizing eyes.

"You didn't eat much tonight," he observed. "Weren't you hungry?"

"I eat mostly vegetarian meals. But don't worry. I can adapt. I'll figure out how to be a rancher's wife if it kills me."

Those words brought Clay up short. As they'd strolled along, he'd almost gotten caught up in this little charade. Having Gaby beside him and cradling her soft hand in his made this concocted relationship seem real. He realized that the lovely Miss Gibson from Atlanta attracted him more than he cared to admit.

He'd been lonely since his divorce from Jill. He hoped someday he'd meet a woman who could share his life. *But it has to be the right woman*, his good sense counseled. And Gabriella Gibson didn't fit his criteria. If he ever married again, it would be to a woman to whom ranch life wasn't alien territory.

As they fell into an awkward silence, Clay realized how tough this game of pretend would actually be. Had they really convinced his men at supper?

Other than a few slips, Gaby played her part well. When she'd covered his hand with hers and said it didn't matter where they were, as long as they were together, her gentle touch made his pulse pound. As this gorgeous, green-eyed creature discussed the marriage that wasn't, she'd almost brought the fantasy to life.

Gaby reminded him of Jill in the early days of their marriage. His ranch hands had treated Jill a little roughly, too, but she'd seemed to adapt well. Clay didn't discover till over a year later that she hadn't adapted at all.

That came as a staggering blow. He'd considered Jill the love of his life. But he'd been wrong.

Dead wrong.

A breeze whispered through the cottonwood trees, freeing a few strands of Gabriella's hair and blowing them into her face. She smoothed them back with a graceful hand. The same hand that had felt unbelievably soft and sensual when tucked inside his own.

Don't be a fool, his conscience cautioned. *Nothing about this situation is permanent*. He'd better not forget that for a single moment.

"We ought to head back," he suggested.

"What's the hurry?"

"We turn in early around here."

"Why is that?"

"Because we get up at four-thirty," he explained, frustrated by the lovely Miss Gibson's total ignorance of ranch life.

Her green eyes widened. "In the morning?"

"Of course, in the morning. We eat breakfast at five."

"And I'm cooking it." Gaby wondered how on earth she'd fry up a cow or two by five o'clock tomorrow morning.

The job she'd accepted suddenly seemed impossible. How could she survive stuck out here in the middle of nowhere, surrounded only by cattle and cowboys? And how could she stay emotionally detached from Clayborne Forrester while trying to convince all these strangers they were married?

When they approached the house, Clay reached for her hand again. This time he threaded his fingers through hers and the fit seemed perfect. Although she tried not to respond to Clay's touch, it was like expecting ice cubes not to melt when dropped into boiling water.

Jackson bounded toward them from behind the barn. "Uh, oh," she said. "Here comes trouble."

Instead of jumping her, Jackson rubbed against Gaby's legs. It was still pretty unnerving. Like being nudged by a freight train.

"Hi, big fella." She slipped her hand out of Clay's and bent to scratch Jackson's head.

The dog's tail whipped her soundly. He made a low, guttural noise that reminded her of the cry of a sea lion.

As she continued petting him, he closed his eyes, basking in the attention.

Moments later, Clay took her hand again and the three of them moved on. They passed the bunkhouse where laughter and the sound of a television blared into the twilight. If any of the ranch hands saw them, they must look like a real family. A rancher, his wife, and their faithful dog.

They were anything but. They were a rancher, his faithful dog, and an actress hired to play a part.

Gaby suddenly thought back to her fifteenth birthday. She'd asked Mama and Daddy for a stereo but hadn't expected to receive one. But they gave her the new sound system, complete with high-quality speakers, and she was thrilled.

She remembered how her parents had stood by smiling, their arms linked around each other's waists. They were still happy together then. It was a treasured memory.

But the happiness didn't last. Things were not what they seemed in the Gibson household. A few weeks later, Daddy left and Gaby never saw him again. That loss still brought pain—and made it very difficult for Gaby to trust men.

Things were not what they seemed between herself and Clay, either. She couldn't afford to forget that fact.

Jackson spotted a rabbit and charged after it, his foghorn bark nearly causing the poor bunny a heart attack. It dashed for cover as Jackson lumbered along behind.

Clay opened the kitchen door where the Formica

counters were all sparkling clean. The heavy smell of fried food still lingered in the air.

Gaby felt edgy. She knew what came next. Clay would invite her upstairs and the two of them would share his bedroom. She swallowed hard as she considered that awesome possibility.

They would argue politely over who slept in his bed and who got the couch. Gaby's throat constricted as she waited for the handsome rancher's unwelcome invitation.

"What's that?" Clay pointed to an envelope propped against a napkin holder in the center of the kitchen table.

"I don't know."

He strode over to pick it up. "Uh, oh. It says 'To the Newlyweds.' What do you suppose it is?"

"You could open it and find out."

But he didn't. He handed it to her. "I don't like the looks of this. My ranch hands are up to something."

Gaby took the envelope and slit it open, then pulled out a note scrawled on a piece of notebook paper.

"Read it," Clay instructed. "Out loud."

She cleared her throat and began to read. " 'After you left, we discussed what to get you for a wedding gift. Jonas thought Miz Gaby might like some new dishes. And Zeb and Zack thought she might like a new picture for the living room. But I said there was only one thing you two needed. A honeymoon.' "

Gaby's throat felt suddenly parched and she paused a moment before continuing.

" 'So we reserved a room for tonight at the Elms Hotel in Denver. Don't worry about getting back early tomorrow. We'll take care of everything. Just have a great time. Love, Zeb, Zack, Randy, and Jonas.' "

The note slipped through Gaby's fingers and fluttered onto the table. While Clay's bedroom had seemed intimidating, it suddenly felt safe. Much safer than a downtown hotel room.

Gaby didn't know what would happen next in this soap opera that had become her life. But she knew one thing for certain. She wasn't going to share a hotel room with Clayborne Forrester.

Not in this lifetime.

Chapter Three

"This is insane," Gaby declared. "We simply can't go."

"We don't have much choice," Clay declared. "It would be rude to refuse their gift."

Gaby whirled to face the handsome cowboy she'd married in name only. "This pretense is hard enough to maintain at the ranch without going public. Besides, I'd never share a hotel room with a man who isn't my husband."

"Now, don't go getting huffy on me, Gabriella. We'll figure something out."

Gaby planted her hands on her hips. "Like what, for instance?"

He shrugged. "Maybe we could stay in different rooms. My hands would never know the difference."

She took a steadying breath. "Can you arrange that?"

"Of course. Go pack a bag. Looks like we'll be taking that honeymoon, after all." He winked at her and the gesture made Gaby's already racing heart beat even faster.

They both headed upstairs to pack and within half an hour were driving toward downtown Denver in Clay's Ford Bronco.

When they entered the expansive lobby of the Elms Hotel, Gaby caught her breath. The high-ceilinged room was filled with rose and blue velour couches and tables of highly-polished cherry. A huge crystal chandelier was the focal point of the ornate room. "This place is magnificent," she whispered.

"It ought to be. The new owners just spent a fortune remodeling."

Clay strode toward the registration desk and was greeted by an attractive, well-dressed woman of about fifty. "Mr. Forrester. How nice to see you again."

Clay set the suitcases down and extended his hand. "Hi there, Mrs. Martin. I'd forgotten that you work at the Elms."

"Sure do. I've just been promoted to night manager."

Clay didn't seem as laidback as he had at the ranch. He ran a hand through his hair, and said, "Then congratulations are in order."

"To you, as well. Randy told me you just got married. When he called to reserve the bridal suite, I was glad it was available."

As Gaby joined Clay at the desk, the hotel manager smiled graciously. "You must be the new bride. I'm Sylvia Martin, Randy's mother."

"Hello. I'm Gabriella Gibson."

"Forrester." Clay shot her a cautious glance.

Gaby giggled nervously. "Forrester, of course. I'm not used to my new name yet."

Sylvia Martin laid a perfectly manicured hand on Gaby's arm. "You'll love our bridal suite, Mrs. Forrester. It has a heart-shaped bed. The only one in town."

"How wonderful." Gaby tried to make appropriate responses while keeping her true feelings of panic and terror under wraps.

"The parking lot looks pretty full tonight," Clay observed.

"With several major conventions in town, every room in the hotel is reserved." Mrs. Martin handed Clay a key, then motioned to a young man in uniform who leaned against the wall and looked bored to tears. "The bellman will take you upstairs."

The fellow sauntered over. Without comment, he picked up their bags and moved toward the elevator.

Gaby's panic and terror intensified. She gripped Clay's arm anxiously. "What about that extra room?"

"You heard Mrs. Martin. The hotel's booked solid."

"But you promised."

Clay turned to her. When his commanding eyes raked over her, her heart skipped a series of beats. "Listen, Gabriella, I'll do anything I can to make your stay in Colorado pleasant. But I can't work miracles. Walking on water and getting another room at the Elms tonight both fall into that category."

He grabbed her hand and led her toward the elevator.

"Besides, how would I explain an extra room to Randy's mother?"

Gaby sighed. She couldn't answer that.

As the elevator transported them to the twenty-second floor, no one said a word. Clay looked uncomfortable and Gaby felt numb with fright. She wished the bellman would say something to break the tension but he didn't. Maybe the fellow was mute, or something.

When the elevator stopped, the bellman led them to room 222 where a bronze plaque beside the door announced: THE BRIDAL SUITE. Gaby's throat tightened in terror. It might just as well have said CHAMBER OF HOR-RORS or STEP RIGHT UP TO THE ELECTRIC CHAIR. Ice water now flowed through her veins.

When Clay inserted the key, Gaby froze. For most couples, unlocking this particular door led to a night of wonder and romance. But for Gaby, it was just the next installment in this nightmare gone berserk.

She started to enter, but before she could manage, the bellman uttered his first words. "It's bad luck, sir, not to carry the bride over the threshold."

"I almost forgot," Clay said gruffly. Then he scooped Gaby into his arms as dramatically as Rhett Butler had scooped Scarlet.

Gaby felt lightheaded from the shock of being crushed against Clay's strong chest. She reminded herself it was all an act but having Clay's arms wrapped around her made it difficult to think straight. She couldn't have felt more excited, or more nervous, if she had been a blush-ing bride.

After crossing the threshold, he set her down. She

struggled to get her balance but felt like a newborn colt whose spindly legs refused to support its weight.

The bellman pointed at the ceiling where Gaby spotted a sprig of mistletoe. Was the hotel going to stage manage their entire honeymoon?

"That's mistletoe." The bellman's smile widened. He was the only person in the room enjoying himself.

Clay stared at the mistletoe as if it were a broken tree limb ready to crash down on their heads. He cleared his throat and moved toward Gaby.

He wouldn't kiss her again, would he? Just because the bellman was pointing at a piece of wilted greenery dangling from the ceiling?

He did. And for the second time in this unbelievable day, Clayborne Forrester's lips claimed hers. For the second time, Gaby's emotions jerked to attention like a car slamming into a brick wall. She felt the rush of a powerful whirlwind sweep through her body, fogging her brain, and sucking the little bit of strength she still possessed right out of her body.

Clay's lips were warm, and moist, and wonderful. In spite of herself, she leaned into him, surrendering to his embrace. For a few magical moments, Gaby let herself get lost in the charade. Clay's mouth covering hers became an all-consuming fire and she forgot all about the bellman. The only thing that mattered at this moment was kissing her pretend husband.

Never had a kiss thrilled her as much as Clay's. And never had a man exuded the sheer sense of power Clayborne Forrester exuded. What would it be like to embark on a real honeymoon with Clay? For a split second, she wished they weren't acting.

He finally broke the embrace but his dark eyes clung to hers even after he backed away. Had the kiss affected him as powerfully as it had her? Had it shaken him to his very foundation?

Don't be ridiculous, her common sense chided. The kiss was for the benefit of the voyeur-bellman who stood grinning like a toothy orangutan.

Clay reached into his pocket and pulled out several dollar bills. Surely he wasn't going to tip the guy? The bellman ought to pay them for their sterling performance.

The fellow grabbed the money and stuffed it into his shirt pocket. "Thank you, sir. Have a wonderful honey-moon." He winked conspiratorially at Clay, then left the room.

Silence reigned as the "bride" and "groom" stood gazing at each other. Gaby took a steadying breath, reminding herself that things were not what they seemed. She was not beginning her honeymoon. She was merely moving into the next scene of this very complicated drama.

But at the moment, moving anywhere seemed out of the question. She felt cemented to the spot.

"Let's check out the suite," Clay suggested.

Gaby forced her legs to carry her into a very large bedroom. "There's the heart-shaped bed," she said in a half-whisper.

The bed, with its ornate brass headboard, was decked with a red velvet spread and adorned with an explosion of white lace pillows. Above it, a flock of golden cupids with filigree wings and little rounded bottoms frolicked joyously together.

Clay's eyes seemed glued to the bed. "It looks like a huge valentine come to life." He shook his head. "I can't possibly sleep in anything this frilly. You take the bed and I'll . . ."

His eyes scanned the room for another piece of furniture that would hold his six-foot-plus frame. There was none. He sighed. "I reckon I'll take the floor."

"You can't sleep on the floor."

"It won't do my back much good," he grumbled. "Yesterday I got tossed by a horse I've been trying to break. But don't worry. I'll manage."

"Maybe there's another room. After all, they call this a suite." Gaby pulled open a door but found only a closet.

Clay whistled in amazement. "Come check out this bathroom. It counts as a room."

Gaby gazed at the mirrors adorning the walls and the ceiling of the huge bathroom. A Jacuzzi surrounded by ferns and candles took up half the room. "It looks like the Hall of Mirrors."

Clay shifted from one foot to the other and Gaby suddenly realized how out of place he must feel in this haven of velvet, cupids and lace. Was he having as much trouble adapting to this impromptu honeymoon as she?

"There's something you should know," he said as they moved back into the bedroom. "I'm a very sound sleeper. I sleep through thunderstorms and golf-ball size hail. So if you need me for anything during the night . . ."

He glanced down at the carpet, then started over. "If

you want to wake me up for any reason . . ." He shot her an embarrassed glance, then cleared his throat. "Well, it might take a bucket of ice water."

"I, I see," she stammered. "Thanks for the warning."

A loud knock startled them both. "Who could that be?" Gaby asked frantically. "People don't usually have guests on their honeymoon."

Clay's jaw tensed. "I wouldn't put anything past my ranch hands."

He strode to the door and opened it. A woman in a black satin dress topped with a crisp organdy apron pushed a cart into the room. "Dessert for Mr. and Mrs. Forrester. Compliments of the Elms."

"Hey, thanks," Clay declared.

The cart, decked with a white linen tablecloth, contained a luscious chocolate torte, two red roses in a crystal vase, and a silver coffee pot. Dishes and silverware were also provided.

"Looks pretty tempting," Clay said as the employee pushed the cart over to the window. The young woman lit two taper candles in brass candleholders.

"If you need anything else, just ring the front desk. Mrs. Martin said to roll out the red carpet for the newlyweds."

As the employee left the room, Gaby wished she could go right along with her. But she couldn't. She had work to do. The work of pretending.

Clay methodically transferred everything from the cart to a small table beside the window. He must not be nearly as unnerved as she. His hands were steady. Even his voice seemed steady. Right now, steady was not an adjective that applied to any part of Gaby's anatomy.

When he finished, the table was perfectly set. He held a chair for her, saying, "We've endured a lot since supper, Mrs. Forrester. Might as well enjoy some dessert."

"I suppose so."

Gaby dropped into the chair, determined to be as matter-of-fact as he. But how could she when this was the most romantic setting she'd ever encountered? The city lights sparkling below them created a totally dreamy atmosphere. Add to that one drop-dead gorgeous rancher, candlelight and flowers, and the stage was set for romance.

For a moment, the fantasy seemed real. If she closed her eyes, Gaby could almost believe this was something other than an out-of-control farce.

"Pretty classy." Clay's deep voice cut into her musings.

Gaby tried to steel herself against the romantic mood. She couldn't let that gorgeous moon and all these accouterments confuse her. After taking a bite of the torte, she found it difficult to swallow. Suddenly her whole body refused to submit to this ridiculous charade.

"I can't do this, Clay," she said, pushing her chair back. "It's a travesty. Your employees spent their hard-earned money to give us this honeymoon and we're deceiving them."

Clay suddenly looked tired. "It's late anyway. Might as well turn in. Would you like the bathroom first?"

His consideration touched her. "Thanks," she said. "I won't take long."

Relief washed over Gaby as she closed the bathroom door behind her. She leaned heavily against it, desperate for a few minutes of isolation. No bellman, no mistletoe, and most important, no handsome, sensual "husband."

She finally opened her overnight case and used some cream to remove her makeup. Then she took down her hair and brushed it a hundred strokes. After slipping out of her clothes, she donned a peach-colored nightgown that was going to clash like crazy with that red velvet bedspread.

Studying her reflection in the mirror, she realized the low-cut gown that hugged her body exposed considerable cleavage. She'd planned to purchase a robe before leaving Atlanta, but ran out of time.

Nothing was working the way she planned. From the moment she climbed out of the taxi at the Silver Saddle Ranch, she'd lost control of her life. She didn't know who was in charge now, but it certainly wasn't her.

Having stalled as long as she could, Gaby sighed and went to rejoin her "husband" in Cupid's lair.

Clay dimmed the lights and stood in the shadows. As he gazed down at the brightly lit city, Gabriella, who'd spent quite some time in the bathroom, came out to join him.

You're a dead man, Clay thought as the angel in peach-colored satin drifted over to stand beside him. Her hair, which hugged her shoulders, shone like a golden halo.

The fitted gown left no question in his mind about the lovely body the bogus Mrs. Forrester possessed. For one ridiculous moment, Clay wished she really was his wife.

He felt sorely tempted to trail his fingers through Gaby's long, silky hair. Fighting off the urge, he jammed his hands into his pockets, afraid they might betray him.

He forced himself to gaze down at the lights of the city. "Pretty, isn't it? While I'd never live in town, Denver has a certain charm. Especially at night."

"Big cities fascinate me," she said softly. "I don't think I'd be happy anywhere else."

"You love Atlanta, don't you?" he asked, searching for a neutral topic.

"Atlanta's a marvelous city. It's retained the grandeur of the Old South while moving into the twenty-first century." She gazed up at him. "What do you think of my home town?"

"Atlanta's a great vacation spot," he affirmed. "Amy and I love to go to Stone Mountain and visit the Swan House."

Gaby's eyes lit with pleasure as he mentioned the familiar places. Atlanta was dear to the lovely lady's heart. "We're very different, you and I," he observed.

"How do you mean?"

Clay pulled one hand out of his pocket, not at all sure that was wise. "Well, I'm a steak and potatoes man and you're a vegetarian. You love big cities and I'd die in the midst of all those skyscrapers. I want to ride my horse for hours and still be on my own property."

Gaby's sigh sounded like a delicate whisper. "I've never ridden a horse. I suppose we are very different." After a moment's silence, she added, "But we're alike in at least one way."

"What's that?"

"We're both committed to our parents," she said. "You've gone to a lot of trouble to make your father happy. You must love him very much."

"I do."

"I understand that. I loved my parents, too."

Clay watched her blink back tears. One escaped to trickle down her cheek and before he could stop himself, his free hand mutinied and brushed it away. "What's wrong, Gaby? Aren't you close to your parents anymore?"

"Mama got sick and died in April. And my father left a long time ago."

"I'm sorry. No brothers or sisters?"

She shook her head.

His pretend wife suddenly looked so vulnerable that it took all the discipline Clay possessed not to gather her into his arms. He fought an overwhelming urge to protect this woman—to kiss away the pain she was experiencing.

He slipped a handkerchief from his pocket and tucked it into her hand.

"Thanks." She dabbed at the tears. "I don't know why I brought this up. I've hardly mentioned Mama's illness to anyone, let alone her death."

"It's O.K. I know how you feel."

"Thanks for understanding."

Gaby blew her nose, then flashed the smile Clay was fast becoming addicted to. The one that made his pulse race, his palms grow sweaty, and a stab of desire spark through his body.

"Guess we'd better change the subject," she said. "It's a grim topic."

"Life's not always upbeat. I'm sorry you lost your mother. Since my Dad's heart attack, I worry a lot about losing him. That's what started this whole marriage scheme."

"You really believe that thinking you're married will please your father?"

"Absolutely. Dad wants my sister and me to have great marriages like his and Mom's, but neither Amy nor I can figure out how. Funny. Our folks make it look so easy."

Gaby suddenly felt unbearably tired. She'd left Atlanta early this morning and had endured incredible stress all day. "What time is it?" she asked, finding it hard to fathom they were still in day one of the charade.

"Eleven-thirty. I guess we'd better go to . . ." Clay stopped. "Well, you know," he finished vaguely.

Gaby felt her face flush. "I found some extra blankets and pillows in the closet. I'll get them." She returned and stacked the bedding on a chair. "Sure you can manage on the floor?"

"I'll be fine."

His willingness to oblige made her feel suddenly guilty. "Since you've hurt your back, I wish you'd take the bed. I'll take the floor."

"It's a big bed." He cleared his throat. "We could probably share it." Before she could refuse, he said, "I promise to keep my distance."

"I suppose we could try," Gaby said hesitantly. But

even as she spoke, Clay's earthy aftershave attacked her senses. She backed against a chair for support.

He strode to the bed and folded down the velvet spread. Then he arranged the lace pillows in a straight line down the center of the heart-shaped bed. Flashing the sexy smile that both excited Gaby and made her anxious, he said, "The boundaries are set. Anyone caught crossing over will be shot for trespassing."

She giggled nervously.

"You can turn out the light now," Clay said quietly.

"How will you see?"

"The lights of Denver provide more than enough light. Besides, there's a huge moon out tonight." His voice reverberated through the room, tugging at Gaby's heart. Moments later, he entered the bathroom and closed the door.

Gaby turned off the lights and crawled into the heart-shaped bed, staying as close to the edge as possible without falling off. The darkness felt welcome. Like a curtain dropping. It carried with it a sense of safety and anonymity.

A short time later, the door opened again. From the shadows, she saw her handsome hunk of a husband emerge. When he climbed into bed beside her, she caught her breath. The room again grew heavy with this cowboy's magnificent scent and presence.

"Sleep well." His deep voice drifted toward her out of the darkness.

"You, too." Gaby turned toward the wall. It took forever for her heartbeat to slow to near normal.

A long time later, Clay's breathing turned steady and

she knew he'd fallen asleep. That helped her relax a little.

Not that she distrusted this great-looking cowboy. While they'd only known each other a few hours, she could tell that Clayborne Forrester was an honorable man. He'd never take advantage of a woman. She sighed. Somehow, that only made the attraction stronger.

Clay woke and felt a warm presence beside him. How could that be? The sensation startled him. He'd been sleeping alone ever since Jill left.

When he glanced at the other side of the bed, all of last night's misadventures came flooding back. Gabriella Gibson lay beside him, one graceful arm resting gently on his chest. As his breathing turned ragged, Clay lay his head back on the pillow, trying to decide what on earth to do next.

Obviously, the border established by the pillows hadn't kept Gaby from trespassing. He lay perfectly still, both tantalized and tortured by her nearness. If he moved, he'd awaken her and he didn't want to disturb her sleep. She'd survived a pretty nerve-wracking day yesterday. They both had.

Pulling his gaze away, Clay glanced out the window, desperate for distraction. A rosy glow edged the horizon and he knew that in just moments the sun would rise. Forcing himself to focus on the outside world, he watched the sun blaze a fiery trail across the morning sky.

The sunrise proved glorious, one of the most intense

he'd witnessed in months. He almost woke Gaby so she could enjoy it with him.

But he had no business waking her. No business being in this bed with her. Gaby didn't belong to him. She was just an actress he'd hired to convince his parents he was a happily married man.

As he lay there, Clay's thoughts drifted back to Jill. He'd adored his wife and thought she was as happy living on the ranch as he. But that, too, had been an illusion. Losing Jill was the biggest disappointment of his life.

If he ever married again, he'd choose a woman well suited to ranch life. And Gabriella Gibson didn't fall into that category. But he couldn't deny that the feelings she stirred inside him were powerful.

Disturbing.

He'd better get out of this bed before he did something stupid. Like pull her into his arms and kiss those fabulous lips that tasted like warm honey.

As he carefully extricated himself from Gaby's hold, she turned over, sighed, and continued sleeping. He went to shower and dress, then returned to the bedroom. Fortunately, he hadn't awakened her.

Clay decided to give his make-believe bride a special present—the gift of privacy. He'd let her awaken and dress without the discomfort of his presence. Jamming the room key into his pocket, he left the bridal suite, gently closing the door behind him.

Chapter Four

Gaby awoke with a start. She'd been dreaming about cattle and Old English Sheepdogs. And about cowboys. One in particular.

She shot up in bed and for a moment couldn't figure out where she was. Then the truth dawned. She was in the bridal suite of the Elms Hotel with Clayborne Forrester, her pretend husband.

There was no sign of Clay. The lacy pillows that formed the border were still in place. Gaby slipped out of bed and tiptoed to the bathroom, relieved to find it empty. Had Clay gone downstairs for a newspaper or some coffee? Wherever he'd gone, she was thankful to be able to shower and dress alone.

An hour later, she heard a key turn in the lock. By then, she'd straightened the room and sat dressed and waiting for him.

"Good morning."

Everything about Clay seemed to have intensified overnight. He appeared taller than ever and looked particularly delectable in a charcoal-gray sweater that exactly matched the color of his eyes. He wore his trademark jeans and boots.

"Good morning," she replied, struggling to keep her voice steady.

"I talked to Mrs. Martin. The hotel's sending up breakfast."

"Breakfast, too? Jonas and the guys went all out on this honeymoon package."

A knock on the door interrupted their conversation and Clay went to answer. A voice announced, "Breakfast for Mr. and Mrs. Forrester."

A middle-aged man in a white uniform wheeled another cart into the suite. "Eggs Benedict, broiled potatoes, and stewed tomatoes," he announced. "Chef's specialty. Hope you enjoy your meal," he said as he left them alone.

"Before we eat, I need to call the ranch," Clay said. "I'm having some wood delivered for the fence and I want to tell Jonas where to have it unloaded."

He picked up the phone and dialed. "Jonas? Clay." He listened a moment, then shot Gaby an embarrassed glance. "Yes, we're enjoying our . . . ah . . . honeymoon very much. Thanks for the great present."

Gaby ignored the thrill that raced through her. Just having Clay's intense eyes focus on her was enough to cause an emotional revolution.

As quickly as he could, Clay switched the subject to

business. He told Jonas about the lumber and seemed about ready to hang up when a shocked expression clouded his handsome features. He rubbed his forehead nervously and asked, "When is she coming?"

After listening for the reply, he added, "Gaby and I will leave the hotel right away. We'll be there as soon as we can."

When he slammed the receiver down and turned to face her, Gaby felt something terrible had happened. So when he said, "We've got to get back to the ranch. We're having company," that didn't sound so awful.

"Company? Who's coming?"

"My sister. Amy's on a business trip and has a four-hour layover in Denver. She's on her way to the ranch right now."

"Uh, oh."

"Uh, oh is right. If she beats us home, our marriage will be instantly annulled."

Gaby sighed. Another dimension of their runaway life was about to catch up with them.

"Pack your things," Clay said. "And grab that chocolate cake. We'll serve some to my sister."

It was with sadness that Gaby left the Eggs Benedict and boiled potatoes untouched. She even felt some remorse at leaving this incredible room. It was probably the first time in its history that nothing had been consummated in the Bridal Suite.

Within minutes, Clay retrieved the Bronco from valet parking and they headed for the ranch. Gaby fidgeted nervously as she sat beside the handsome cowboy she'd just honeymooned with. Even though their relationship was purely platonic, a new intimacy seemed to exist between them due to their intimate sleeping quarters.

Lying awake beside Clay last night, his strong body just a touch away, had wreaked havoc on her emotions. How would it feel, she'd wondered, to stroke his arm, or trail her fingers over his muscular chest? To experience the prickle of his dark beard, or place a gentle kiss on his cheek?

"So what's our game plan?" she asked, pushing those stimulating thoughts aside.

"To stop Amy before she tells the truth about us."

Gaby shook her head. "Your sister will think we've lost our minds."

His grin was wry. "And she's probably right."

As they drove along, Gaby couldn't help admiring Clay's strong profile. A strand of jet-black hair slipped across his forehead, giving him a boyish charm. Just looking at him turned her emotions to putty.

She'd always hoped to marry, but never a man like Clay. Her fantasy man was a successful banker or architect who left home each morning in a tailored suit. One who came home each evening and loved attending the theater and other cultural events as much as she did.

Nope, no cowboys for her, she reminded herself sternly. She wouldn't let this rough-and-tumble man, no matter how appealing, interfere with her dreams.

They drove a while in silence. Then Clay said, "I didn't come up with this pretend-marriage scheme impulsively. My father's chances of recovery are pretty slim. I thought if something made him really happy it might improve his frame of mind. Maybe even his chances."

"I hope you're right," Gaby said quietly, realizing how important his family was to Clay. "Tell me about your father."

A kind of peace filled his eyes as he began to talk. "He's a rancher, through and through. Dad owned the Silver Saddle for thirty years. Then five years ago, he sold the spread to me. But he kept ten acres to build a log cabin. He and Mom lived there until they decided to move to Florida. That hasn't worked out well for Dad. I suspect he's bored to tears."

"Maybe he needs a hobby."

"The folks play shuffleboard and Mom drags Dad off to Bingo several times a week. But I think he's homesick for the mountains and desperately misses the ranch."

"Does your mother realize he's unhappy?"

"I don't think so. Dad calls me while Mom's out shopping. Even before the heart attack, Dad struggled to adjust. He says he's seen so much sand and sunshine that he feels more like a beachcomber than a cowboy."

"What about golf? Lots of retired people love to play golf."

"Dad says he'd like golf better if he could ride a horse from hole to hole, instead of one of those flimsy golf carts."

She chuckled. "I like your father already."

"He'll like you, too, Gaby. And so will Mom."

Why did those casual remarks send such joy arcing through Gaby? Clay wasn't saying *he* liked her. Just that his parents would.

He's paying you to make his folks believe you're their daughter-in-law, she reminded herself. She bit her lip, reminding herself this was a job. Not a relationship.

As they turned onto the dirt road leading to the Silver Saddle, dust billowed into the open windows of the Bronco. Gaby sneezed one of the violent allergy sneezes that shook her entire frame. Then another, and another.

"Roll up your window," Clay instructed as he rolled up his own. Then he flipped on the air conditioner. "Does that help?"

She gratefully inhaled the filtered air. "Oh, yes. Thanks."

He flashed a crooked smile. "Not much of an outdoorswoman, are you? Every little speck of dust makes you sneeze."

She sniffed indignantly. "I love the outdoors. I don't have this much trouble in Atlanta because we cover our dirt with grass or concrete. It's more civilized that way."

His mouth curved into a tantalizing smile that made her heartbeat accelerate. "You're impossible, Gabriella."

Gaby tried to ignore the sensual way this cowboy pronounced her name. And the fact that she felt giddy as a schoolgirl sitting here beside him.

Clay pulled the Bronco up to the ranch house. "Uh, oh. Looks like we're too late."

"How do you know we're too late?" she asked.

"There's a car out front I don't recognize. Probably Amy's rental car."

Gaby's stomach knotted. If Amy had told Clay's hands the truth—that she'd never heard of Gabriella Gibson—their game of pretend was over. Funny, she didn't want it to end. Not yet. "What do we do now?"

"Try to salvage what's left of our marriage."

If that's possible, Clay thought as he grabbed the torte and escorted his pretend wife inside. They found Jonas and Amy chatting in the entryway. "How's my favorite sister?" he asked, breaking into their conversation.

Amy turned and smiled. "Clay! We haven't seen each other since . . ."

"Since February," he interjected. He gathered Amy into his arms, praying she wouldn't correct him. In truth, they hadn't seen each other since Christmas.

"Go along with me, Sis," he whispered. "I'll explain later."

Clay stepped back, hoping Jonas hadn't already discovered his marriage to Gaby was a farce.

Amy's dark eyes widened and she looked confused. "I had a layover and couldn't resist visiting my kid brother."

"Hi, Amy," Gaby interjected. "I didn't realize we'd see each other quite so soon."

Amy's mouth dropped open and her eyebrows raised. "Um, me either. This is certainly a surprise."

"How long have you been here?" Clay probed, trying to gauge how much time Amy and his foreman had to converse.

"I just arrived. Jonas said you spent last night in Denver."

"Is that all he said?"

Amy nodded. "I told you I just got here."

Clay expelled his breath slowly as relief kicked in.

Maybe it wasn't too late. "We have some exciting news," he told his sister. "Gaby and I got married day before yesterday."

"Married? You got married?" Amy's eyes widened so much that her eyebrows disappeared beneath her bangs. A stunned smile covered her face and she wasn't blinking.

Gaby rushed to his sister's side. Throwing her arms around Amy, who wasn't moving or blinking, she said, "And it's all thanks to you."

"It is? Well, well, well." Amy's voice register sounded higher than usual.

To his sister's credit, she didn't say, "Who are you, anyway?" She just kept smiling and saying, "Well, well, well."

"If we hadn't met at Gold's Gym in Atlanta last winter," Gaby said pointedly, "you'd have never introduced me to your brother." She drew a deep breath and continued. "Why if it weren't for you, Amy, Clay and I would never have gotten married."

"Glad to be of service." Amy looked like she'd progressed from surprise into shock.

"Let's head for the dining room and have some of the torte Gaby and I brought back from our honeymoon."

"Honeymoon. So you went on a honeymoon." Amy's smile looked flash-frozen to her face.

"Jonas and the boys gave us a night at The Elms as a wedding gift," Clay told his stupefied sister.

"How nice. How nice."

Amy's dark eyes held a vacant look and she was saying everything twice. She'd turned from a witty, clever conversationalist into one of the Stepford Wives.

"Jonas, would you put on a pot of coffee?" Clay asked.

As his foreman left the room, Clay grabbed one of Amy's arms and Gaby took the other. They commandeered her into the dining room, where she dropped into the chair Clay pulled out for her.

While Gaby retrieved the cake and set it in the center of the table, Clay sat down across from his shell-shocked sister. "I know this comes as a surprise."

Amy expelled a breath. "That's an understatement. It's hard enough to believe you've remarried, Clay. But what's all this about Gaby and me knowing each other?" She hesitated, then glanced at Gaby. "Your name is Gaby, right?"

"Right."

"I'll start at the beginning," Clay volunteered, but at that moment Jonas returned, carrying a tray that held plates and forks as well as cups of steaming black coffee.

"I'd just perked a fresh pot, so we're all set," his foreman announced. For once, Clay was sorry Jonas was so darned efficient.

As he started serving slices of the torte—their wedding cake, of sorts—Jonas turned to Amy. "Were you as surprised as I was to learn these two eloped?"

"More so," his sister retorted. "I still can't believe it."

Their confusing conversation lurched along with a series of jagged starts and stops. Fortunately, Amy let Clay and Gaby do most of the talking. When they finished eating, Jonas said, "I need to run into town and pay some bills. If you'll excuse me, I'll get moving."

As soon as Jonas left, Amy said, "All right you two, what's going on here?"

Clay started talking. First he told Amy of his concern for their father's health. "You know how Dad's always wanted us to be happily married. Since we both tried and failed, I decided to hire a pretend wife."

Amy quirked an eyebrow. "So you're not married." She paused a moment, then said, "At least that's creative."

"The folks are coming for a visit," Clay continued. "I figured my being married would please Dad."

Amy sat quietly pondering the new information. Then she smiled. This time her smile seemed genuine rather than flash-frozen to her face. "Maybe your little plan will work, Clay. It's certainly worth a try."

When Clay glanced at Gaby, she flashed that tantalizing smile. The one that made his pulse pound like the hooves of a skittish colt. This woman fascinated him. She brought life to the ranch in much the same way Jill had.

And remember how badly that turned out, he reminded himself. The pain of Jill's leaving had put a permanent scar upon his heart. But he couldn't entirely blame his ex-wife. He should have realized she wasn't cut out to marry a rancher. He should have recognized the signs.

The signs were certainly clear where Gaby was concerned. The woman was totally mismatched to ranch life. That would help him keep his perspective. And remember that she didn't belong here any more than Jill had.

* * *

"I hope I didn't give anything away," Amy said as Gaby and Clay walked her to the rental car.

Gaby squeezed Clay's sister's hand, realizing she liked this woman a lot. "You're a better actress than I am. If you want to try out for any plays in Atlanta, I've got connections."

"I'll remember that. How long will you stay at the ranch, Gaby?"

"Just till your parents leave. Maybe you and I can really meet for lunch when I'm home again."

Amy smiled. "I'd like that."

Clay hugged Amy and they said their goodbyes. Gaby sensed that this brother–sister relationship was especially close.

How wonderful to have a sibling that you cared about the way the two Forresters cared about each other. Gaby looked on with a touch of envy, wishing she had family to share her life with.

But she didn't. No brothers or sisters. Even her mother had died. Gaby was the last remaining Gibson—other than her father. Heaven only knew where he'd ended up.

"I've been worried about Dad, too," Amy confessed, "so I hope your plan works. Keep me posted." Then she turned back to face Gaby. "As pretend sister-in-laws go, you're a gem. Clay got lucky when he married you."

The comment touched Gaby, and for a moment she felt part of this family gathering rather than just an envious bystander. "Thanks. That means a lot."

Amy reached out and gave Gaby a quick hug, then

climbed into the rental car and maneuvered it onto the dirt road. They waved until she drove away.

"Your sister's sweet," Gaby said.

"She seemed to like you, too. Amy's not usually so friendly to a stranger."

A stranger. The word pulled Gaby up short. She shivered as the false sense of belonging vanished. She wasn't part of the Forrester family, and all the pretending in the world wouldn't change that. A heavy sadness enveloped her as she and Clay walked toward the ranch house.

"Have you got a minute?" he asked. "There's something I want to show you."

"You're the boss." Gaby reminded herself sternly that that's *all* he was.

Clay escorted her across the field toward the corral. Several horses pranced around its periphery. "Do you see that mare? The chestnut-colored one?"

Gaby caught her breath as she looked at the stately animal. "Oh, yes. He's magnificent."

Clay chuckled. "It's a mare, Gaby. A female horse."

"Oops, sorry. *She's* gorgeous."

"Her name is Cinnamon. And she's yours."

"She's mine?"

"You'll need a horse while you're here."

"But I don't know how to ride."

"You'll want to learn. You may never visit a ranch again."

The word "visit" again reminded Gaby of her status at the Silver Saddle. "Actually, I hadn't given it much thought," she said, hiding her disappointment. "Cinnamon seems awfully big. Do you have something in a smaller size?"

"She's not so big. The two of you make a good match."

The horse suddenly picked up its gait and began trotting around the corral. "Then how about something with a little less horsepower?"

Clay chuckled. "She's just showing off. Trying to impress you. Want a riding lesson?"

"How would I get up there? With an extension ladder?"

Smiling, Clay reached out and smoothed back a strand of Gaby's hair that had slipped out of the bun. The tender gesture made her heart race. "You won't need a ladder, babe. I'll teach you everything you need to know."

His comment and gentle touch made Gaby tingle. For a moment, she wanted Clay to teach her more than just how to ride a horse.

"So how about it? Tomorrow's your first lesson."

She shrugged. "Sure, why not."

When the matter was settled, Gaby sighed. Riding a horse, especially the tall, stately animal Clay had chosen for her, seemed as impossible as pulling off their pretend marriage.

Learning to ride a horse would require great concentration. Maybe that would take her mind off her cowboy husband and the attraction that grew stronger each passing hour. Just looking at him as he stroked Cinnamon's silky neck, brought Gaby a rush of pleasure. The feelings Clay stirred surprised her by their intensity.

How different this Colorado ranch was from her life

in Atlanta. If she were there now, she'd be escorted to all the summer plays and musicals by Brett Logan, a banker she'd been dating. She wouldn't be trying to figure out how to ride this stately horse without breaking her neck. Or how to curb her attraction to this great-looking cowboy.

A stab of homesickness hit her as she wondered what happened to her former world. It suddenly felt light-years away.

The memory brought her to her senses. She must keep her relationship with Clay platonic. She'd play the role he'd hired her to play, then return to her real life.

The one that had nothing to do with cowboys.

That evening, Gaby and Clay relaxed in his living room, reading the newspapers. But because of Gaby's intense attraction to her rancher husband, nothing she read transferred to her brain. The newsprint contained a conglomerate of vowels, consonants and punctuation that held no meaning whatsoever.

Clay sat stocking-footed, with one long denim-covered leg resting on the other. That was all she could see of the man, with the exception of two broad, strong hands which held the *Denver Gazette*. But the image was still sexy. Gaby knew darn well what a well-toned, muscular body lurked behind that newspaper.

He seemed lost in thought. How could he concentrate on the outside world when all Gaby could think about was the events transpiring at the ranch?

This was the second night in a row that she would sleep in the same room with Clayborne Forrester. Last night, in the bridal suite of the Elms Hotel; and tonight in his very own bedroom. At least here they'd have separate beds, and wouldn't have to deal with candlelight and mistletoe.

Clay folded the paper and laid it aside. "Ready to turn in?"

She glanced at her watch. "It's only nine o'clock. I haven't gone to bed this early since I was in third grade."

He stretched, reaching his flannel-covered arms toward the ceiling. "Don't forget you're cooking breakfast tomorrow," he reminded, his slightly-sleepy voice sounding sexier than ever. "The fellas expect to eat at five o'clock sharp. They're building a fence and will need a hearty meal."

Gaby groaned and laid her portion of the newspaper aside. "Clay, I don't know if I can handle this job. My biological clock operates on a different time schedule. I stay up till midnight and sleep till eight."

"It's just your second day. You'll adapt."

"What will I feed the hands for breakfast?" she asked, half-afraid to hear his answer.

"Nothing fancy. Just scramble a couple dozen eggs, whip up a big stack of pancakes, and fry several pounds of bacon. And be sure to make plenty of strong, black coffee."

"That sounds like it would feed a small village."

"Don't worry. I'll help out until you get the hang of it."

"You will? Gee, that's terrific."

When he grinned, Gaby felt another jolt of pleasure.

It wasn't only Clay's magnetic smile that worked magic on her heart. His thoughtfulness did, too.

He got to his feet, his sexy, stocking-clad feet, and extended his hand. "So shall we, um, go up to bed, Mrs. Forrester?"

His dark eyes held a teasing glint and Gaby struggled to keep her hormones under control. "I am kind of sleepy. It's nervous exhaustion. I've been on edge since the moment I arrived."

His smile vanished. "This job isn't intended to be an exercise in torture, Gabriella. You've got to relax."

"How can I relax? Every time I start to, someone asks another question I can't answer. Like 'Where was the wedding?' Or, 'Who stood up with you?' Or, 'How long did you and Clay date before you married?' " She sighed heavily.

"I told you this job wouldn't be easy. But with your theater background, I assumed I was hiring a professional."

"This kind of acting is so different," she lamented. "Usually, I memorize a script and nothing changes. Here at the ranch, I ad lib every minute."

I'd better lighten up, Gaby realized. Clay suddenly looked worried about their undertaking. Flashing him a smile, she said, "If I'm not careful, the truth might slip out."

His jaw relaxed a little. "We can't have that. Come on, wife. Let's get some sleep. Things will look brighter in the morning."

As he steered her upstairs, a butterfly invasion landed

in Gaby's stomach and took up residency. Clay's hand on her arm felt warm and delicious.

Once again, Gaby reminded herself this was all pretend. That was tough when this cowboy's smile and touch seemed genuine. If she closed her eyes, she might convince herself this really was their honeymoon—that she and Clayborne Forrester truly loved each other. That their relationship was more than a bizarre game of "Let's Pretend."

She gave herself a mental shake. This man was her employer, for Pete's sake. Not her husband.

Clay stopped in the hallway. "The bedroom's all yours. I'm going to take a shower. It helps me relax."

When he disappeared down the hall, Gaby shed her clothes and slipped into her gown in record time. Under no circumstances did she want Clay to catch her in her underwear! Or worse!

After brushing her hair, she grabbed sheets from the closet and made up a bed on the couch. She grabbed a novel from her suitcase, and lay down. Compared with the wonderful bed at The Elms, the couch felt like a bed of rocks. She spent the next several minutes trying to find a comfortable position, finally realizing that comfort and this lumpy couch were mutually exclusive.

She started reading, hoping it would take her mind off both the uncomfortable couch and the fact that she was again sharing a bedroom with this drop-dead gorgeous cowboy.

A knock on the door interrupted. "Come in," she called.

Clay entered, dressed in pajama bottoms with a towel

draped around his shoulders. Unfortunately, the towel didn't cover enough of his muscular chest to do much good. His tanned skin was covered with a generous sprinkling of dark curly hair and just looking at the man caused a wild flutter in her pulse.

"You take the bed, Gaby." He winked at her. "If you don't get adequate rest, you'll be demanding a raise first thing tomorrow morning."

"But, I . . ."

"No buts. Now move."

The bed did look incredibly inviting after the miserable minutes she'd spent on this broken-down couch. "O.K. But tomorrow night we'll trade."

"Fair enough."

As she moved from the couch toward the bed, Clay's hand brushed Gaby's arm, causing another surge of pleasure. She felt like one of her high-school students whose emotions resided in their fingertips. The girls' lives were a roller-coaster ride of hormonal highs and lows. Much like hers had become since she'd arrived in Land's End, Colorado.

At that moment, Clay's eyes locked with hers, setting up a magnetic field that held them together. He took a step backward. Had he experienced the same kind of electric charge?

"Do you . . . um . . . need anything?" he asked.

"Not a thing."

"I'll leave the night-light on. In case you get up for any reason."

"I won't be getting up," she said. "Not for any reason."

"O.K., then. Goodnight." Clay switched off the light, bathing the room in blissful darkness.

Gaby had just started to relax when his deep voice boomed at her from the other side of the room. "I've never slept on this couch before. The springs shoot out in all directions."

"I noticed."

"Maybe if I change positions." The couch creaked and groaned beneath his weight. He tossed a bit longer, then said, "Nope. Position has nothing to do with it."

"I noticed that, too. But I won't feel sorry for you again and invite you to share my bed. Don't even think about it."

"It's actually my bed."

"Well, I'm borrowing it."

He sighed heavily. "Have you no mercy, woman?"

"None, whatsoever."

Gaby could picture Clay peering at her from the darkness. When she remembered his sore back, she almost weakened. But not quite. She couldn't spend another night in the same bed with this handsome cowboy unless circumstances were different. Unless. . . .

She didn't want to think about it.

Chapter Five

Gaby was midway between sleep and wakefulness
when she first heard it. Glass shattering. Then what
sounded like the crack of thunder. She sat up in bed, a
sense of dread attacking the pit of her stomach. "Clay!"

No answer.

Next came whoops and hollers and horrible screeching
noises. It sounded like an Indian raid. "Clay! Wake up!
Wake up!"

Still no response.

A horrible thought struck her. Maybe someone had
slipped into the bedroom and killed her pretend husband.
Otherwise, he'd surely have heard her cries. After all,
she was screaming at the top of her lungs.

Gaby tossed back the covers and ran to the couch.
Clay's body was limp. One arm dangled lifelessly to the
floor, one leg flopped over the arm of the couch. She

grabbed his shoulders and shook him, desperate to see some movement. In the meantime, the outdoor noises continued.

"Clay! Clay!" she called. He lay there limp as a rag doll.

Trying frantically to recall the instructions for mouth-to-mouth resuscitation, she leaned over him and pinched his nose shut. Then she placed her mouth over his and blew the breath of life into his body.

Breathe. Clay, breathe. She continued the mouth-to-mouth resuscitation, disgusted with herself for the surge of pleasure that Clay's still-warm mouth stirred. She must be part ghoul!

After considerable effort on her part, Clay moved. Then he sat up and rubbed his eyes. "What in blazes are you doing?"

"Thank goodness! You're alive and breathing."

He stared blankly. "Of course, I'm breathing. I've done it all my life."

Now that he was out of danger, Gaby remembered the disturbance outside. "Someone's breaking into the house," she declared. "Quick, get your shotgun before they come upstairs and murder us in our beds."

"I don't have a bed," he growled. "Just a couch. Now what makes you think someone's breaking into the house?"

The breaking of glass had stopped and the shrieking had died down. Gaby now heard a different noise. It sounded like singing! Like *very bad* singing!

Clay struggled to his feet and went to peer out the

window. He sighed in disgust. "That figures. It's my ranch hands."

"Your ranch hands? Have they lost their minds?"

"Not entirely. I suspect they're throwin' us a shivaree."

"A shiver what?"

"A shivaree. Don't tell me you never heard of a shivaree?"

"Is it some sort of dread disease?"

"A shivaree is a celebration for newlyweds. Friends of the happy couple break dishes on their front porch and make a gosh-awful racket. The goal is. . . ." He hesitated a moment, then continued. "The goal is to disturb the bride and groom during their. . . ." He cleared his throat and added, ". . . lovemaking."

Gaby felt heat creep into her cheeks. She shuddered as she again realized the misconception in Clay's men's minds. They believed she and Clay were husband and wife in every sense of the word.

"Actually, it's quite harmless," Clay said. He flipped on the light and went to raise the shade. "Come over here, Gaby. Where they can see you."

"I will not."

"Do you want these clowns howling out there all night?"

"Heavens, no."

"Then do as I say."

Clay opened the window and Gaby reluctantly went to stand beside her hunk of a husband. He slipped a toasty arm around her waist and pulled her close, making her pulse rate skitter. While she tried to ignore his strong, muscular body, it was like ignoring an erupting volcano.

When the ranch hands saw the happy couple, the singing stopped. They started clapping, cheering, and whistling instead.

"Your singing wasn't half bad," Clay called to the crooners. "Maybe you can get a job at the 'The Longbranch Saloon.' Considering you're now unemployed."

Noisy laughter followed.

"If you've finished the serenade, or whatever you call it, maybe my wife and I can get some sleep."

"You don't know much about shivarees, do you, boss?" one of the cowboys called.

Clay sighed. "What are you driving at, Zeb?"

"There's only one way to shut us up."

"And what's that?"

"Feed us, of course!"

Clay rubbed his forehead and groaned.

"What's wrong?" Gaby asked

"We have to feed these characters. Gosh dang, we'll never get any sleep." He stuck his head out the window. "We'll meet you in the kitchen in five minutes." As the cowboys cheered, Clay slammed the window.

"Now what?" Gaby asked.

Clay glanced at his pretend wife and sighed. Gabriella looked deathly pale and was shivering. He glanced at the delicate gown she wore and decided it exposed more of her enticing body than he wanted exposed. No way was she going downstairs looking like that. "Did you bring a robe?"

A blush tinted her cheeks. "I planned to buy one before I left Atlanta, but I ran out of time."

He strode over to the closet. "Here. Wear mine."

His oversized robe nearly swallowed Gaby up. But at least Zeb, Zack, and Randy wouldn't spend the next half an hour staring at his pretend wife. Funny, how protective he felt toward Gabriella Gibson after only two days of "married life."

She belted the bulky robe, then glanced at him with those lush green eyes. "What will we serve? I rarely entertain people in the middle of the night."

"There's still some torte left. And we'll pop some corn."

"It's not like they'll starve to death. We'll be feeding them breakfast in a few hours." Gaby sighed. "Taking care of your hands is like having three giant children."

Clay grinned as he slipped into his jeans and pulled on a T-shirt. "Come on, honey. Let's go feed the kids."

Once again, they all gathered around the trestle table—with the exception of Jonas, who was older and had more sense. Clay poured soft drinks and started the corn popping while Gaby sliced the torte.

"I hope our little serenade didn't disturb you," Zeb said pointedly.

"Or interrupt anything," Zack added. "We planned to serenade you at the Elms last night, but Randy's mother said our singing wasn't up to hotel standards." This comment brought a big laugh from his cohorts in crime.

Clay saw a flush reappear on Gaby's cheeks. "All right, you characters. No more crude comments in front of my bride."

When Gaby shot him a grateful glance, Clay felt a rush of pleasure. It seemed he and his make-believe wife could already communicate just using their eyes.

After the men downed the refreshments, their noisy enthusiasm began to subside. Being awake after midnight was a departure from these cowboys' normal routine.

"Around here, a couple isn't considered married till they've been shivareed," Randy observed.

As Clay slipped an arm around Gaby's shoulders and pulled her close, her delicate scent mesmerized him. She leaned into him and her body felt delicious against his. "Did you hear that, honey? We're official now."

She sighed. "I certainly hope so. I wouldn't survive another shivaree."

With the appetites of his voracious hands assuaged, Clay herded Gaby back upstairs. She crawled back into his bed and Clay tried to ignore how sensual it was to have this enticing woman snuggling between his sheets.

He took his place on the couch. "The barn dance is tomorrow night. Still want to go?"

She yawned. "Do you think it's a good idea?"

"You wanted to meet some other women. Now's your chance."

"Won't it make things harder if we're seen in public? Shouldn't we keep our relationship a secret?"

He chuckled. "A secret? Why, Sylvia Martin's informed half the state of Colorado by now."

"Oh, dear. I'd hoped we could keep this marriage in house."

"Just because we're secluded at the Silver Saddle

doesn't mean there's no communication. A grapevine runs through this part of the country that rivals the gossip column in any New York City newspaper."

Gaby sighed. "Then we might as well go. What should I wear?"

"A dress with a full skirt. One that will twirl real pretty when we dance the Virginia Reel."

Clay switched off the light. " 'Night. Sleep tight."

" 'Night, Clay."

Her drowsy voice tugged at him—made him wish he had the right to crawl into his bed and gather the sleepy, sexy Gabriella Gibson into his arms. He could imagine how perfectly her body would mold to his; how sweet her hair would smell; how delicious her lips would taste. And for one crazy moment, he wished things were different between them.

This was the second night he'd tried to fight off his runaway attraction to this woman. Early this morning, he'd taken a long walk to regain his perspective. Waking up in bed with Gaby so tantalizingly near had been more than one red-blooded cowboy could endure. He'd wanted to reach out and stroke her shiny hair that fanned across the pillow.

Instead of doing something stupid, he'd gotten up, showered and dressed, and walked all over downtown Denver, lecturing himself about not becoming emotionally involved. It was downright stupid to get caught up in this simulated marriage.

He was preaching himself the same sermon tonight but it wasn't working. Not until he remembered what happened when he fell in love with a woman who didn't love the ranch. Losing Jill had brought incredible heartache.

That thought sobered him fast. He'd be a fool to make the same mistake twice in the same lifetime.

"Gabriella? Gabriella?"

The voice barely penetrated Gaby's consciousness. She raised her head to see who was speaking from the darkness in such a deep, commanding voice. Was it God?

"The bathroom's free," the voice boomed.

If it was God, his message wasn't very profound. She snuggled back into the pillow. "That's nice."

"Get up, Gaby. It's 4:15."

Recognition dawned though daylight hadn't. The low-pitched voice belonged to Clayborne Forrester, her pretend husband. "We've got to get breakfast started," he rumbled. "I'll go down and start the coffee. You won't fall asleep again, will you?"

" 'Course not."

"Promise?"

"Mmmmm hmmmm."

The room grew blissfully quiet and while Gaby's mind told her to get up, her body wouldn't cooperate. It was marvelously dark in the room and wonderfully warm in Clay's comfortable bed. She drifted back into a dream in which she was starring in a play. She'd just stepped forward to take a curtain call when . . .

"Gaby! You went back to sleep! My men will be here in twenty minutes expecting breakfast."

Reluctantly, she threw back the comforter. "I'll be right down."

Clay disappeared into the hall, but not before he flipped on the light, flooding the room with brightness. Obviously, he didn't trust her to stay up.

Rightly so.

She threw on a pink sweater and a pair of gray slacks, then hurried to the bathroom to splash cold water on her face and brush her teeth. She made it downstairs in four minutes flat. Of course she probably looked like she'd been on an all-night binge.

"You can start the bacon," Clay instructed as Gaby stumbled into the kitchen.

The man was not only wide awake, but also looked terrific in a red T-shirt and jeans. His dark hair shined and he'd already shaved. How could anyone look so sexy before sunrise?

Gaby shuddered as she picked up the limp strips of bacon. Facing raw meat first thing in the morning was a shock to a dedicated vegetarian. Somehow, she managed to arrange the bacon in the skillet and soon it sizzled in chorus with Clay's perking coffee.

She studied the strips with dismay. Not because of her eating preferences, but because they had more energy than she did.

"Shall I scramble the eggs now?" she asked.

"Good idea. I set the cartons on the table."

Gaby stifled a yawn as she cracked eggs into a large mixing bowl. They stared up at her like a mass of eyeballs with giant yellow pupils. She had to get more sleep. She was losing touch with reality.

Grabbing a whip, she beat the eyes—eggs—thoroughly. "Where's your Pam?"

He stopped his work to glance at her. "My Pam?"

"You know. The stuff you spray onto a skillet to keep the eggs from sticking."

"My eggs never stick. I fry them in bacon grease."

"Oh dear." She tried not to sound horrified. But for a vegetarian frying anything in bacon grease was heresy.

It's part of your job, she reminded herself and dutifully fried the eggs in the awful-looking stuff.

A short time later, Gaby detected the smell of burning food. "Are your biscuits burning?" she asked Clay.

He strode across the room and peered through the glass on the oven door. "Nope. They're not quite done."

Gaby suddenly realized what was going up in smoke wasn't the biscuits. "It's my bacon!" she yelled.

He rushed over and jerked the skillet off the burner but it was too late. The bacon, that a short time ago had been limp and sickly looking, was reduced to brittle charcoal. "Oh, dear. I got busy scrambling and forgot all about it."

Clay grabbed a spatula and scraped the charred remains of his hands' breakfast into the garbage disposal. "They'll have to get along without bacon this morning."

"I'm really sorry."

While Gaby did look penitent, Clay couldn't help wondering if she'd burned the bacon on purpose. After all, she was a vegetarian.

"Don't worry," he mumbled. "We'll manage."

His imaginary wife stood beside the stove, hands on her slender hips, eyes big as sand dollars. Even with disheveled hair and no makeup, Gabriella Gibson was a sight to behold. He could stand here staring at the woman all morning long.

Dragging his gaze away, he determined that today Gaby wouldn't turn his emotions topsy-turvy.

Zeb opened the door and stepped into the kitchen. "Mmmmmmm. Smells great in here. Can't wait to sink my teeth into that bacon."

Clay ignored the comment. He'd let the truth sink in gradually.

The others took their places at the table and greeted Gaby warmly.

She beamed at them. "Morning, fellas."

"Can't wait to sample your cooking," Randy replied.

Clay poured coffee and Gaby set the eggs and biscuits on the table. "You forgot the bacon," Zeb observed.

Gaby cleared her throat. "I didn't forget the bacon. Actually, I burned it."

Zeb's face fell. "You burned the bacon?"

"Listen, I'm really sorry." Her green eyes looked huge and repentant.

For a moment, silence reigned. Then Zeb said, "We don't like bacon all that much anyhow."

The blatant lie made Clay realize that his hands had wholeheartedly accepted Gaby. Enough to sacrifice one of their favorite foods.

It would be tough for them when they learned the truth—that he and Gaby were just pretending. His hands enjoyed this woman's presence at the ranch. To be honest, so did he.

"I'll do better tomorrow morning," Gaby promised,

flashing her captivating smile. "Here, Zeb, help yourself to the scrambled eggs."

"Don't mind if I do, ma'am." Zeb loaded his plate with eggs and never said another word about the bacon.

That evening, Gaby and Clay entered a huge brick-red barn filled with people and bales of sweet-smelling hay. The screeches and squawks of a fiddle being tuned mingled with sounds of congenial conversation.

As Gaby inhaled deeply, her lungs filled with the pungent scents of musty wood and damp straw. Why had she wanted to attend this dance? Weren't things complicated enough without involving the neighbors in their little charade?

"Howdy, Clay." An auburn-haired woman dressed in a red checked blouse, flared denim skirt, and tan leather boots hurried toward them.

Clay gave her a casual hug. "Hi, Adrienne. I see you've packed the place, as usual. When you and Jack throw a party, folks drive in from all over the county."

"We love a crowd. The more the merrier."

Gaby waited to be introduced but Clay said nothing. Finally, she placed her elbow gently in his ribs.

"Oh, um, Adrienne," he stammered, "I want you to meet Gaby, my . . . my wife. Honey, meet our hostess, Adrienne Mason."

Would Clay ever be able to say the word wife without tripping over it?

Gaby smiled at their hostess. "Nice to meet you, Adrienne."

"You, too, Gaby. We got word yesterday that you two

had eloped. Frankly, it's going to take a while to forgive you for sneaking off like that. Folks around here look for any excuse to celebrate. And weddings top our list."

Clay shrugged and twisted the brim of his Stetson in his hands. "Sorry to disappoint you, Adrienne. But Gaby and I wanted a quiet affair. No fuss."

Their hostess looked as if she couldn't quite fathom that. "We'll forgive you eventually. Now go and mingle. Everyone's dying to meet your new bride."

The next few minutes passed in a blur. Clay introduced Gaby to so many people she couldn't begin to keep them all straight. Everyone seemed pleasant and friendly.

A cowboy, who stood on a platform at one end of the barn, grabbed a microphone. "Howdy, folks. As most of you know, I'm Jack Mason and I'll be your caller tonight. Before we begin, I have an announcement. Clay Forrester, the most eligible bachelor in the county, just got himself hitched. Everyone be sure and meet Clay's new bride Gabriella."

Cheers and shouts filled the barn. Clay grinned and pulled Gaby close, sending more sensations of delight coursing through her body.

"O.K., let's form our squares," the cowboy instructed. "I'll walk you through 'Brown-eyed Sue.' "

Before Gaby knew what hit her, she and Clay were part of a square. His strong arms guided her as Jack called out each new step. Dancing with her bogus husband proved a stimulating experience. Having Clay's arms around her for any reason increased her heart rate and set off an endorphin explosion of monumental proportions.

Gaby soon learned her new husband was a great dancer and an excellent teacher. Without his guidance, she'd never have survived the first dance.

"Swing that pretty gal round and round," Jack called. When Clay held her closer still, Gaby's heart took off like a greyhound at the starting gun. His warm breath tickled her neck, sending thrills sparking through her body. Just being near Clayborne Forrester turned Gaby into a dreamy-eyed adolescent.

I'm in big trouble, she thought anxiously. She must learn to keep a healthy distance from this attractive rancher while still pretending to be his wife. How stupid of her not to realize that a barn dance wasn't conducive to keeping Clay at a distance.

"Next, we'll dance to the Cowboy's Serenade," Jack instructed. As he walked them through it, Clay's masculine scent caressed Gaby's senses just as surely as his muscled arms corralled her body.

After another half hour of dancing, Gaby felt as if the barn were closing in on her. She glanced at a door people had been slipping in and out of all evening. "I need some air," she said. "Why not dance with someone else till I get back?"

Clay looked perplexed. "You sure?"

"Positive. Enjoy yourself."

Gaby threaded her way through the crowd, feeling ready to snap from the tension. The claustrophobia brought on by the crowded barn and the confines of her pretend marriage nearly overwhelmed her.

She stepped gratefully into the cool evening air and inhaled deeply. Spotting a tree swing a short distance away, she hurried toward it.

The sun had set and the bright moon provided a soothing wash of light. As she sank gratefully onto the swing, she heard the fiddle music in the distance. From here the muted sounds proved much less agitating.

The clean, mountain air revived and refreshed her and some of the tension slipped away. The stars looked like handfuls of diamonds tossed over a black velvet quilt. Gaby sighed, letting the movement of the swing and the comforting darkness work their magic on her tattered nerves.

Pretending to be Clay's bride was getting tougher by the hour. From the first moment he swept her into his arms, Gaby's heart was off and running. And it hadn't stopped. She never dreamed playing this role would be so difficult.

And the acting wasn't the biggest challenge, she realized. Clayborne Forrester's tanned, muscled body was the biggest challenge. Whenever any portion of it came into contact with her own, all thoughts of pretending vanished.

You're letting your emotions take charge, she scolded. Roping herself one Colorado cowboy was not on her agenda now and never had been. She thought back to her recent dates with Brett Logan. Brett loved the theater as much as Gaby did. The past few months, the two of them had shared some pleasant evenings together.

But she didn't react to Brett's kisses the way she did

to Clay's. They didn't cause shivers of delight to ripple through her body. Or make her long for more.

If this pretend marriage was to work out, she'd have to get her emotions in line. Make certain they didn't usurp her common sense.

"Are you all right?"

A deep-pitched, masculine voice cut into Gaby's thoughts. And the peace she'd regained slipped away like water trickling down a drain.

She slowed the swing and sprang to her feet. "Clay. You startled me. It's beautiful out here, isn't it?" she said, struggling to collect her thoughts. "I was getting pretty warm inside."

"Same here. I just danced the California Jig with Jennifer Dawson. It's a real lively number." Clay slipped a bandanna from his pocket and mopped his brow.

Gaby felt a sudden twinge of jealousy. "So you did find another partner," she said, a little disappointed that he had. "Is Jennifer Dawson one of the rancher's wives?"

"No. Jen's not married."

Gaby had seen lots of children and adolescents as part of the sets. "Is she one of the teenagers?"

He chuckled. "Jen's hardly a teenager. She and I dated for a while. When you left, she asked me to dance."

"I see."

Well, Clay's old girlfriend hadn't wasted any time, had she? As feelings of jealousy tugged at Gaby, she fought them off. Who Clay danced with—even who he'd dated—was none of her concern. She'd only be in his life a few days before returning to Atlanta.

Clay looked more handsome than ever with the moonlight shadowing his features. "The stars look unusually bright," she observed, forcing her attention away from Clay's powerful physique to something larger—like the universe.

"It's the mountain air. Not much pollution around here."

"That explains it. And the moon's still full. Even fuller than it was on our . . ." She paused, unable to complete the sentence.

". . . on our honeymoon. You can say the word. We both know it wasn't real."

For some reason, that comment hurt. A cool breeze rustled the leaves and Gaby shivered. "You're cold," he observed. "Did you bring a sweater?"

As Gaby shook her head and turned her back to him, Clay realized how vulnerable she looked. The woman was far from home and friends, living a pretend life. Before he could stop himself, he stepped forward and placed his hands on her shoulders.

That didn't seem to help. She shivered even more. So he slid his hands up and down her arms to increase the circulation. Touching Gaby always took his breath away.

She stiffened at his touch and he wished he'd had sense enough to keep his hands to himself. "Want to go inside?"

She hesitated a moment, then nodded.

But he couldn't let her go. The dark sky lit by the golden moonlight, the gentle breeze teasing Gaby's skirts, and the feel of her soft skin beneath his hands held him captive.

"Are you sorry you came to Colorado?"

"No. I'm not sorry."

"Why did you take this job?"

She sighed. "For Mama. She was sick almost a year. And while she had insurance, she still ran up some big debts. I couldn't pay them on my salary alone." Gaby was silent, then added, "This job means a lot to me."

"Funny. We're both doing something deceptive for our parents' sakes."

She shrugged. "I guess people do strange things for the ones they love."

Clay felt goosebumps ruffle the smooth texture of Gaby's arms. "You're cold. Let's go inside."

When she turned to face him, the nearness of her body stirred a fire inside him. Clay couldn't clearly distinguish Gaby's features in the dim light, but that didn't matter. He'd memorized them the first afternoon she arrived. Her stunning eyes, slightly Patrician nose, and heart-shaped mouth were forever engraved in his consciousness. Leaning closer, he placed a gentle kiss on her lovely mouth.

At first, she didn't respond, but when he deepened the kiss, Gaby moaned softly and leaned into him. She wrapped her slender arms around his neck and stepped into the embrace, pressing her marvelous body firmly against his own. He didn't dare move, hardly dared breathe, for fear she'd pull away.

The wind picked up, whipping at Gaby's skirts. Strands of her hair blew against his face. It felt silky— like angel hair.

The desire inside Clay swelled dangerously. He knew how foolish this was, knew he ought to stop, yet couldn't. For several moments, they lost themselves in the wonder of each other. Time ground to a halt and Clay wished this moment could stretch on forever.

Suddenly Gaby pulled back and caught her breath. "What are we doing? You and I can't afford to get caught up in this charade."

Clay filled his lungs with the fresh mountain air and tried to clear his confused thoughts. "You're right," he said quietly. "Let's head back."

As they started walking, Clay chided himself for coming outside in the first place. He should have stayed indoors with Jennifer and played it safe.

Running a hand through his hair, he wondered what was happening to him. He'd always been a single-minded man. He'd always set a goal and worked toward it. And his goal in hiring Gaby was to help his ailing father, not to get sidetracked by this woman, no matter how tempting she was.

Gaby caused the same kind of passion inside him that Jill had aroused. But passion wasn't enough to keep a relationship alive and strong. People had to want the same things from life. Jill was sorely mismatched to the lifestyle he adored and that ruined their marriage.

So is Gaby, he reminded himself sternly.

Better watch it, Forrester, his good sense cautioned. *You can't afford to fall in love again.*

Certainly not with Gabriella Gibson.

Chapter Six

The barn loomed ahead like a safe haven in the impending darkness. While Gaby had been anxious to escape it earlier, she now felt glad to return. Being alone with Clay had proved disastrous.

As soon as they entered the barn, an attractive, dark-haired woman approached them. She wore a calico dress with a tight bodice and flared skirt that showed off a most impressive figure. Sinfully long eyelashes shrouded her dark-brown eyes and her skin looked smooth as satin.

The woman laid a possessive hand on Clay's arm and flashed a radiant smile. "There you are, darlin'. Did I wear you out dancing the California Jig?"

"We needed some air." Clay seemed oblivious to the way the woman clutched his arm. Or the way she tried to ensnare him with his eyes. "Jennifer, have you met my wife Gaby?"

The woman's eyes dimmed considerably. "Haven't had the pleasure. I'm Jennifer Dawson, Clay's former girlfriend."

Gaby forced a smile. "Nice to meet you."

Jennifer shifted her attention back to Clay. As she monopolized him, at least they didn't have to tell any more lies about the marriage that wasn't. This woman couldn't care less about Clay's marital status.

Jack's voice blared over the microphone. "All right, gang, grab your best girl for the Sweetheart Waltz. No squares this time."

Clay took Gaby's hand. "Excuse us, will you, Jennifer?"

The woman placed a finger over her lips. "Oh, listen, Clay. They're playing our song."

Clay looked perplexed.

"Don't you remember? This is the number the band played the night we won the dance contest."

"Oh, yeah. I'd forgotten."

"Gaby, honey," Jennifer said, syrup literally dripping from her words, "would you mind terribly if I dance this with your husband? It holds so many memories."

Clay started to object but Gaby intervened. "Go ahead, sweetheart. I'll share you with your old flame for one last dance." Gaby put extra emphasis on the word old.

Clay shrugged and relented. "Come on, Jennifer. Let's see if we've still got it."

"Oh, we've still got it, honey. Trust me."

Annoyed and frustrated, Gaby sank onto a bale of hay. Thanks to Jennifer, the barn wasn't proving a safe haven

at all. She couldn't wait to escape this barracuda in calico.

As she watched Clay and Jennifer dance, she noticed
that their bodies moved in perfect rhythm. Jennifer
looked enchantingly happy. To Gaby's chagrin, so did
Clay.

Everything about Jennifer Dawson annoyed Gaby.
Even her style of dancing. She moved in a slow and
sensual manner—as if she were performing some ancient
fertility rite. Gaby sighed, trying to suppress the jealousy
bubbling inside her.

While she found Clay's former girlfriend annoying,
something troubled her even more: the kiss she and Clay
shared out by the swing.

The other times he'd kissed her he'd had valid reasons. He'd been trying to convince others—first Jonas,
then the bellman—that they were husband and wife.
Those kisses, while much more stimulating than Gaby
cared to admit, were part of the charade.

But tonight's kiss was different. There had been no
bystanders to impress. Clay kissed her because he
wanted to and that frightened her. But what frightened
her even more was she wanted to kiss him right back.

The sensation of the cowboy's strong hands on her
arms had started her heart pounding so wildly she'd
thought he could hear it. Even though she'd tried, she
couldn't make herself pull away from Clay's magic
touch.

She again glanced at Jennifer and Clay, reminding herself that this woman played a legitimate role in his life,
even if that role was ex-girlfriend. Her own status with

the man ranked lower than ex-girlfriend. She was an actress, hired to play a part.

That realization hurt much more than it should.

The following afternoon, Clay came toward Gaby leading two saddled horses: Cinnamon, the chestnut-colored mare she'd met yesterday, and a luxurious, coal-black animal. The entourage stopped directly in front of her.

Gaby sighed. "Cinnamon looks taller than ever. Did you bring that ladder?"

Clay tipped back his Stetson. "You won't need a ladder. But a pair of jeans would have helped. I told you to wear your jeans."

"These are my jeans." Gaby turned sideways, stuck out one hip and pointed to an insignia directly over her back pocket. "See? It says Levi's."

"I didn't know they made white jeans," Clay declared. "Well, they won't be white after we finish riding."

Cinnamon flared a nostril, snorted and stamped her foot. "Dirty jeans are the least of my worries," Gaby affirmed.

She felt a panic attack coming on. If only something would intervene so she wouldn't have to go through with this riding lesson. Where were all the natural disasters when you needed one? Like earthquakes? Or pestilence? A powerful thunderstorm would do. She glanced at the sky, which was robin's egg blue—not a cloud in sight.

"I ought to tell you that the last horse I rode was secured to a circular platform. It turned while calliope music played in the background."

Clay shot her a teasing glance. "You won't find any carousels on a ranch, Gabriella. Now come on. Hang onto the reins, then put your right foot in the stirrup and swing your left leg over Cinnamon's back."

Gaby rubbed her hands together and took another hesitant glance at Cinnamon.

"Mounting's simple," Clay told her. "Watch."

The horse stood perfectly still while Clay swung his agile body into the saddle. The effortless way he mounted emphasized the strength and grace of his tall, lean body. Gaby watched him with admiration. "You make it look so easy."

"It is easy." He dismounted just as smoothly and stood holding the reigns. "Now it's your turn."

Gaby looked up at the horse, who whinnied loudly. "She doesn't like me."

Clay sighed. "How do you know?"

"I just know. Can't we do this some other time, Clay? Please?"

As she turned away, Clay grabbed her arm and twirled her to face him. "I promise you'll be safe, Gaby. What's the matter? Don't you trust me?"

"Gosh, no. And I don't trust that horse, either."

Clay's eyes lit with new determination. "It's time to quit stalling and get on this horse."

There seemed no escape. "What's that little round thing called again? That I'm supposed to put my foot into?"

Which will be the first step in committing suicide.

"A stirrup."

"A stirrup." Reluctantly, Gaby slid her foot in place.

"Now swing your left leg over Cinnamon's back. And put some energy behind it."

Gaby felt sure it would be easier to mount a bird in flight, but she gritted her teeth, closed her eyes and flung her leg as hard as she could fling it. Unfortunately, she overcompensated and nearly slid down Cinnamon's other side.

Clay grabbed her leg. "Whoa, babe. I didn't say pretend you've been shot from a cannon."

Clay's hand on her thigh momentarily eased her fear of riding. Gaby forgot everything except how thrilled she felt each time he touched her. In this pretend world they'd created, Gaby couldn't count on much. The only given was that Clayborne Forrester's touch always left her disoriented and breathless.

Adjusting her body in the saddle, she said, "Maybe this is enough for today."

His reassuring pat increased the tingling sensation which now ran unchecked through her body. "There's nothing to be afraid of, Gabriella."

Chastising her rebellious hormones, Gaby tried to focus on the lesson. "Not for you, maybe. You've ridden since you were a kid. But I've never done this before. I feel like I'm teetering on Pike's Peak."

"Here, take the reins. They'll give you a sense of security. If you want Cinnamon to go left, tug on the left rein. Vice versa if you want her to go right."

"Equestrian blinker lights. Pretty clever."

He grinned and the sparkle in his dark eyes lit a flame in Gaby's heart. "You're impossible," he said.

"Riding's impossible," she retorted.

Clay mounted the black horse just as easily as he'd mounted Cinnamon. "What's your horse's name?" Gaby asked.

"Ranger. Now push your heels gently into Cinnamon's sides."

Gaby nudged the horse with her heels and it moved forward. "Kind of like shifting her into drive."

"You could say that. Now we'll circle the corral until you get used to Cinnamon and she gets used to you."

The two horses moved toward the corral. Since this placed Gaby close to Clay, she felt reasonably safe.

"How are you doing?" he inquired after their first trip around the corral.

"Not terrible. At least, I haven't fallen off yet."

"That's a good sign."

By the time they'd circled several times, some of Gaby's panic subsided. Cinnamon responded to her gentle proddings and her tugs on the reigns.

Mounted on Ranger, Clay looked like the perfect cowboy. His plaid shirt and jeans emphasized his great build, and Gaby admired the adept way he handled the horses. Surely, this rugged outdoorsman could protect her from any misfortune.

He pushed back his Stetson. "Want to take a ride?"

"We are taking a ride."

"I mean live dangerously. Break away from the corral."

"You think I'm ready?"

"Sure. Let's go."

As Clay moved Ranger toward the open field, he glanced back at Gaby, who wore those inappropriate white jeans and a pained expression. She clung to the saddle horn for dear life. "You're doing fine," he told the Atlanta beauty he'd hired to play his wife. But she looked totally out of her element. Like a displaced person.

Their pretend marriage wasn't going as well as he'd hoped. Nothing about Gaby fit the image of a rancher's wife. Her clothes weren't appropriate, she couldn't quantity cook, and riding a horse proved an exercise in torture.

She was, however, a sight to behold. Her jade-green blouse accented her tantalizing figure and brought out the deep green of her eyes. She'd worn her hair loose today and it shimmered in the bright sunshine. If beauty were the criterion for this pretend marriage, Gaby would beat every woman in the county. Hands down.

But beauty wasn't the criterion. Acting experience and knowledge about ranch life were. And Gaby came up sorely lacking.

She sat stiffly in the saddle. If the lovely lady fell off, she'd break every bone in her body. "You O.K.?"

"I'm fine."

Her blonde hair blew into her eyes. Gaby let go long enough to tuck a strand behind her ear, then gripped the saddle horn again.

They crept along at a snail's pace for nearly half an hour. "There's a creek, ahead," Clay said. "We'll give the horses a drink."

"Does that mean I can get off?"

"For a little while."

"Good."

Clay nudged Ranger and his horse picked up speed. Gaby and Cinnamon followed suit. They were finally moving a little faster. He hoped it wasn't too fast.

At that moment, a dog darted out of the underbrush, barking ferociously. Cinnamon whinnied and threw her mane.

"It's the Johnsons' dog, Shiner," Clay called over the noise. "Pull on the reins, Gaby."

Cinnamon whinnied again and Shiner kept right on barking.

Gaby shot Clay a look of sheer terror. "What did you say?"

"Pull on the reins!"

Shiner kept up the chase, nipping at Cinnamon's hooves the same way he nipped at the tires of Clay's truck. "Get back, Shiner," Clay bellowed but the dog continued his vigilant pursuit. Cinnamon threw her mane, whinnied again, then took off at a dead run.

In a matter of seconds, Cinnamon and Gaby left the yipping mongrel far behind. Clay dug his heels into Ranger's sides and took off after them. Gaby's shrieks had now replaced Cinnamon's whinnies.

It took several minutes to reach them. When Clay finally did, he inched Ranger as close as possible and grabbed for the reins. "Whoa, Cinnamon. Whoa, girl," he soothed. But the horse paid no attention.

After several attempts, he brought Cinnamon to a jerky halt. Sliding off Ranger's back, he went to help Gaby dismount. She tumbled breathlessly into his arms. The sensation of her body against his made him breathless, too.

"I got so scared, I forgot everything you taught me," she panted. "I didn't know whether to pull to the left, or pull to the right, or dig in my heels, or . . ."

As he held Gaby close, her body again molded perfectly to his. Her heart beat an irregular cadence against his chest. "It's O.K.," he said, trailing his fingers through her silky hair. "You were doing fine till Shiner showed up."

As Clay held Gaby in his arms, his own heart began to pound. While Gaby's pounded out of terror, his accelerated heart rate was due to her nearness. When she didn't resist, or make any attempt to move out of his embrace, he continued to stroke her hair, thrilled to have her resting against him. While Gaby failed at every ranch-related duty, the woman felt like heaven in his arms. She smelled like wildflowers and summer sunshine.

"You'd better divorce me," she murmured into his shoulder. "I can't cook and I can't ride a horse. I'll never make it as a rancher's wife."

While he agreed, he couldn't tell her so. "It takes time to master the art of riding."

"I don't want to ride like a professional. I just want to feel in control of the horse and not vice versa."

As Clay rubbed the small of Gaby's back, she inched closer. "Cinnamon got spooked, that's all. Next time will be easier."

"Next time? You mean I have to do this again?"

She glanced up at him, her green eyes round and enticing and troubled. And her lips, those luscious, slightly-moist lips, well within kissing range. Clay longed to lower his head and taste them.

He'd kissed her several times now, and each kiss had aroused him more than the one before. Gaby's kisses proved addictive.

Using all the resolve he could muster, Clay forced himself to resist temptation and focus on the purpose of this outing. "With a little time, you'll be riding like a pro."

She shook her head. "That would take days, possibly weeks. I want to impress your parents but I need more time." She sighed deeply. "Maybe you'd better hire a different wife."

He compromised. Instead of kissing her lips, he gently kissed her forehead. "I don't want a different wife. I want you."

Clay's words sent an electrical charge zigzagging through Gaby's body. He wasn't going to fire her in spite of her mistakes. She vowed to try twice as hard.

Clay stepped away from her and took a deep breath. "I'd better give these horses a drink." As he led Ranger and Cinnamon through the grass toward a flowing stream, Gaby held back. She sat on a rock and watched.

Sunshine flooded the June morning. A Monarch butterfly flitted from flower to flower. The valley, lined with snowcapped mountains, looked majestic and peaceful. As the minutes passed, the picturesque scene began calming Gaby's ragged nerves.

She watched the horses drink from the crystal-clear water. "What a beautiful spot," she called to Clay. "Too bad you can't get here on the freeway."

He chuckled. A moment later, he came and dropped beside her in the sweet-smelling grass. "Surely you don't prefer the noise and commotion of highway traffic to riding a horse?"

"I feel in control behind a steering wheel."

"You'll learn to ride, Gaby."

"I suppose."

Several moments passed in silence as they enjoyed the pastoral scene. "It's gorgeous here."

He nodded. "Remember when I told you there was nothing I'd rather do than ride my horse for miles and miles and still be on my own land?"

"Are we still on your land?"

"Uh huh."

"Guess I married myself a mighty rich rancher."

He shrugged. "I do all right. I never have to worry about paying bills or my men's salaries. And I could comfortably support a family—should the need arise."

Gaby perked up her ears. It was the first time he'd mentioned a family. "Will you marry again, Clay?"

"Maybe. If I find a woman who loves living on a ranch. And knows how to pitch in and do the work."

"Did your ex-wife love the ranch?" The question, which was none of Gaby's business, just slipped out.

Clay's expression darkened. "Jill was a city girl. But I thought she'd grown to love the Silver Saddle as much as I did. Unfortunately, I was mistaken."

"I'm sorry," Gaby said, knowing her question had touched a nerve.

"Yeah. So was I."

Clay got up and strolled toward the horses that now

grazed contentedly. He spoke gently to Ranger and stroked his nose, then did the same with Cinnamon.

Gaby again realized how different she and Clay were. This rugged cowboy was perfectly at ease around these magnificent animals that so intimidated her. He loved the wide open spaces, the glorious mountains, and the clear, rushing streams. She sighed, feeling horribly out of place.

Her forte was the big city. She adored bustling downtown Atlanta, and shopping in the thriving metropolis. And she loved the cultural aspects of city living.

Each day it became more clear that she and Clay wanted different things from life.

A little while later, Clay led the horses toward her. "Ready to head back?"

She bent to pick a wildflower, then shielded her eyes from the bright sunlight as she gazed at Clay. "If you don't mind, I think I'll walk."

"It's a mighty long ways. Maybe you'd like to ride with me. On Ranger."

"Is that possible?"

"Sure."

"Who gets the saddle?"

"I do. You can sit just in front of it."

"Won't I fall off?"

"No, silly. I'll hold onto you. Real tight."

Just thinking about having Clay hold onto her real tight again set off sparks of longing inside Gaby. Though she tried to keep her distance from this rugged cowboy, it seemed she was always placed in close proximity to his irresistible body.

But she had to get back to the ranch somehow. "O.K. Let's give it a try."

Clay helped her onto Ranger, then mounted behind her.

"What about Cinnamon?" she asked.

"She'll follow along behind."

Gaby tried to hold her body rigid—to stay as far from Clay as possible. She was managing relatively well until Ranger suddenly lurched forward and Clay's arms tightened around her.

A thrill of pleasure surged through her body.

Why oh why couldn't she disconnect her emotions for the remaining days at the ranch? Sort of unplug them from the rest of her body? Or become immune to this cowboy's charm, strength, and masculinity?

But that was impossible. She'd have to be dead to be immune to Clayborne Forrester's charms.

"What happened?" she asked breathlessly.

"Ranger stepped in a gopher hole."

Gaby swallowed hard. "Does he do that often?"

"Relax, Gaby. Leave the driving to me."

She sighed. "I think I will."

Her willpower suddenly dissipated like dew on a rose. In spite of good intentions, she snuggled into the comfort of Clay's embrace.

Leaning against his strong chest was like leaning into sheer power. Being so close to him made her blood race and filled her with longings she had no business experiencing.

Even if she didn't have a prejudice against cowboys, which she did, Clay had just told her he'd never get involved with a woman who didn't adore the ranch and know how to pitch in and do the work.

That description left her out of the running.

When they reached the ranch, Clay dismounted and helped her down. "We'll have another lesson soon."

"No hurry," she said, not anxious to repeat the experience.

Clay slipped off his Stetson and smoothed his hair. "My folks arrive tomorrow afternoon. We'll head for Denver about three o'clock to meet their plane."

Gaby suddenly remembered why she'd come. For a job. An acting job. "Do you think we're ready?"

"Of course, we're ready," he affirmed.

But he didn't sound convinced.

And why should he? Her success at adapting to ranch life was pathetic. The shivaree gave her heart failure, she burned the ranch hands' breakfast, and she'd just flunked her first riding lesson. Cinnamon should have kept right on running.

Clay seemed to read her thoughts. "I know this has been a struggle for you, Gaby. But if you just pretend you love me, Mom and Dad will forgive anything else."

As he turned and led the horses toward the barn, Gaby sighed. If that was all she had to do, she could manage just fine. Unfortunately, pretending she loved Clayborne Forrester wasn't the least bit difficult.

Chapter Seven

"Ready to head for the airport?" Clay asked. He stood at the bedroom door, dressed in a pair of jeans, a beige turtleneck, and a tweed sports jacket with leather patch pockets. The man looked totally terrific.

"Almost." Glancing in the mirror, Gaby layered yet another layer of mascara onto her thoroughly coated eyelashes.

"We're getting a late start. I don't want my folks to think I've abandoned them."

"Let's go." Grabbing her purse, Gaby went to join Clay.

He smelled of soap and the outdoors. As usual, her heart pounded wildly when she got anywhere near him.

His dark eyes flashed obvious approval. "It was worth the wait. You look calm, collected, and terrific."

"It's all a front. Inside, I'm jittery, anxious, and scared silly."

His crooked grin set her emotions tumbling all over each other. Delight, longing, and fear all merged into a hodgepodge of feeling.

Clay cleared his throat. "Guess I'm a little nervous myself. Taking the Missus to meet my folks is a big step." As they walked down the stairs, he said, "Let's drive the Lincoln today. We'll be more comfortable."

"The Lincoln? You have a Lincoln?"

"I use it for special occasions. But I much prefer my Bronco."

He led her to the detached garage and backed out a luxurious forest-green automobile. "What a beautiful car," Gaby said as Clay helped her get in. "There's a lot about you I don't know."

He winked, which spurred another adrenaline rush. "You'll learn. We've only been married a few days."

Gaby sighed. "This is the most frightening part of this charade. We've been able to convince your employees and your friends, but your mother? She'll take one look and realize I'm an impostor."

Clay patted her knee and let his hand linger as they pulled onto the highway. "Calm down, Gaby. Mom has no reason to suspect."

Her cowboy husband's warm touch had the dual effect of elevating both Gaby's pulse and her panic. "But mothers are intuitive. When I was a kid, Mama always knew when I was telling a fib."

"How'd she manage that?"

"She said it was written across my forehead."

Clay chuckled. "Your mother sounds like one savvy lady."

"She was."

They drove a while in silence. Then Clay said, "Tell me more about your life, Gaby."

"My real life? Or my pretend life?"

"The real one."

"Well, I love teaching. I have a great apartment, and lots of friends—close friends."

Clay quirked an eyebrow. "What about men? Do you date?"

The personal question made Gaby squirm. "Of course, I date."

"Any serious relationships? Is there one special man in your life?"

Other than you?

The thought jumped unsolicited into Gaby's brain and she tried to shake it off. "Sort of," she said. "I've been dating Brett Logan, a banker from Atlanta. We have a great time together. He loves the theater as much as I do."

His hand still rested lightly on her knee and the sexual tension of that gesture threatened to overwhelm her. She twisted sideways, hoping he'd take the hint and move his hand, but he didn't.

"Are you serious about the guy?"

Good question. "Brett and I have a lot in common."

"That's important. The problem with Jill and me was that we were too different. Two people have to want the same things out of life."

"So you don't believe that opposites attract?"

"They attract, all right. But couples that are too different are headed for trouble."

Then Gaby was in trouble. Big trouble. She and Clay were as different as two people could be. And she'd never felt attracted to any man like she did to her bogus husband.

To be honest, her interest in Brett Logan had dimmed since she'd met Clay. That made her uncomfortable. Brett met all her criteria for the perfect man—until she met a certain cowboy who made her question what the perfect man really was.

Gaby was glad when they reached the airport. They hurried toward Terminal A, arriving at the appropriate gate as passengers began filtering into the waiting area.

Gaby bit her lip as she watched Clay search for his parents. Life at the Silver Saddle Ranch was already complicated. And in just moments she'd add a set of in-laws to the complicated puzzle.

The real test lay just ahead. Could she play the role of Clay's wife believably enough to convince his parents?

Maybe she could. Her feelings for Clay grew stronger each day. That should make the playacting more believable. But she'd better take her emotions firmly in hand. This was a short-term "marriage" and nothing more.

"There they are!" Clay grabbed Gaby's hand and pulled her toward an attractive, dark-haired woman pushing a silver-haired man in a wheelchair. The man, pale and drawn, was obviously in poor health.

"Mom! Dad! It's great to see you." Clay embraced his mother, then bent to hug his ashen-faced father.

Clay's mother kissed his cheek. "You too, honey."

"We'll let the crowd thin out before we get your luggage," Clay suggested.

He took over pushing the wheelchair and the four of them moved out of the crowd. As they settled away from the noise and bustle, Clay turned to face his parents. "I have a surprise I've been saving for your arrival. I want to introduce you to a very special lady. My wife Gabriella."

Hearing him speak those words made Gaby tingle. And they made Mrs. Forrester smile. "Your wife?" she declared. "Oh, Clay, what a wonderful surprise!"

"I'm happy to meet you." Gaby extended her hand and Mrs. Forrester squeezed it.

Clay's father's countenance brightened immediately. "You mean my son actually got himself married? She must be one incredible lady to lasso this reluctant cowboy."

"She is, Dad. She's incredible, all right."

Those words didn't help Gaby's composure the least little bit.

"Welcome to the family." The kindly man with dark eyes so like Clay's smiled at Gaby from his wheelchair.

"Thank you, sir," she said, feeling touched by his genuine welcome. But a wave of guilt washed over her as she realized their deception had reached a new height.

On the ride back to the ranch, the car filled with lively chatter. For a few moments, Gaby let herself pretend that she belonged to this incredible man—that she was part of the Forrester family.

Be careful, her conscience chided. She forced herself to think about Brett and reminded herself that he was her type of man. Brett loved the big city and all that came with it.

Ranches and cowboys weren't her forte. She'd do well to remember that.

Barbara Forrester added spaghetti to a pot of boiling water. "How do you like cooking for a bunch of starving cowboys?"

Gaby smiled as she stirred the spaghetti sauce. "It's challenging. They have huge appetites."

"That's for sure. I relied on a formula when I cooked for our ranch hands. First, I figured out how much I thought they would eat. Then I doubled the amount."

Gaby chuckled. "I'll remember that. Did Clay tell you that our hands are eating in town tonight so we can have a quiet family dinner?"

"Isn't that sweet? As rough as our cowboys were, they had hearts of gold."

"Would you taste this sauce, Mrs. Forrester? I'm not sure if it's seasoned properly." Gaby held a spoonful out for Clay's mother to sample.

"Mmmmmm, very good. Maybe a touch more oregano."

"Done." Gaby sprinkled the herb into the mixture and continued stirring. "Now why don't you sit down and relax. I didn't intend for you to work on your first afternoon at the ranch."

"This isn't work, Gabriella. I love helping out. Jill wouldn't ever . . ." She hesitated, then said, "Never mind. That's water under the bridge."

Clay's mother went to sit at the trestle table and Gaby poured them each a cup of coffee. The older woman looked troubled for the first time since her arrival. Joining her, Gaby said, "You can talk to me if you like."

Mrs. Forrester sipped her coffee, then said, "I always liked Jill. But she kept me at arm's length. I'd have loved to pitch in and help cook a meal, but she wouldn't allow it. Sam and I would sit in the living room reading magazines until it was time to eat."

Gaby nodded. "I can see where you'd feel left out."

"Jill meant well but I felt more like a guest here than family." She squeezed Gaby's hand and her radiant smile returned. "I've really enjoyed cooking with you this afternoon. Makes me feel right at home."

"Good." As Gaby smiled at Clay's mother, another surge of guilt attacked her. She was giving this trusting lady a totally false impression.

"I suppose you and your mother do lots of things together."

The pain of losing Mama tugged at Gaby's heart. "We used to. But my mother died recently."

Mrs. Forrester reached for Gaby's hand and squeezed it. "Oh, honey, I'm so sorry."

Gaby tried to suppress the deep sense of loss. "She'd been ill for some time."

"Forgive me for bringing up such a sad subject."

"Actually, it's nice to talk to someone about Mama. She loved to cook. We often baked bread together on

Saturday afternoons. Working with you reminds me of the time I spent with her."

Clay's mother smiled. "That's a compliment I'll long remember."

The sauce bubbled over and Gaby went to turn down the heat.

"Maybe I'd better check on Sam," Clay's mother said.

"Go ahead. Everything's ready except setting the table, and I can handle that."

As Gaby cleaned the stove, she felt relieved the sauce had boiled over. Heart-to-heart talks with Clay's mother might not be such a great idea. If they got too close, it would make Gaby's leaving even harder.

Clay strode in the back door, slipped off his Stetson, and hung it on a peg. His grin sent a thrill sparking through Gaby's body. All the man had to do to set her emotions churning was show up.

He ran a hand through his hair. "How's it going?"

"Supper's almost ready. Your mom helped me cook and we had a nice talk."

The grin widened. "That's terrific."

As Gaby poured the spaghetti sauce into a large serving bowl, her anxiety increased. "Is it? The closer your mother and I become, the harder it will be for you later."

He laid a hand on her shoulder and his touch proved both comforting and stimulating. While the gesture bolstered her spirits, it stirred feelings she didn't want to experience. "I don't care what happens weeks from now, Gabriella. Not even days from now. I just want my parents' visit to be happy. I'll deal with the consequences later."

Gaby sighed. If only it were that simple.

"Now, what can I do to help?"

"Want to set the table?"

"Sure."

As he retrieved dishes from the cupboard, Gaby realized that Clay wasn't like any man she'd ever met. No task seemed too trivial for him. Not even setting the table. She sighed. He'd make some woman a great husband.

That thought made her unbelievably sad. While she knew Clay wasn't the man for her, picturing him married to someone else hurt more than it should have.

Mrs. Forrester pushed the wheelchair into the kitchen. "Something smells wonderful," Clay's father observed as he moved over to sit at the table.

Gaby set the serving bowls in place. "Nothing fancy. Just spaghetti."

Mrs. Forrester joined her husband. "Don't let Gaby fool you, Sam. I sampled her spaghetti sauce and it's delicious."

Gaby warmed to the praise. When everyone's plates were filled, Barbara Forrester said, "Now tell us all about the wedding. Did you get married in a church or elope?"

Gaby and Clay's eyes met as they decided who would speak first. "We went to a wedding chapel in Denver," Clay finally said.

Barbara turned to Gaby. "May I ask if you've been married before, Gabriella?"

She couldn't quite meet Barbara's gaze. "No. This is my first time."

"Too bad you kids didn't have a big church wedding

with all the trimmings," Sam added. "You'd make a gorgeous bride, Gaby, in one of those fancy satin dresses."

Clay looked at Gaby and squeezed her hand. "Gabriella was a gorgeous bride," he said. "Even without the fancy gown."

While she hadn't been able to meet Barbara's gaze, Gaby couldn't seem to resist Clay's dark, sensual eyes. They made her feel like a starry-eyed adolescent. And the hint of desire sparking from his gaze excited her all the more.

"Thank you, honey," she said, trying to make the appropriate response without succumbing to his abundant charms.

Sam Forrester leaned forward. "Did you take a honeymoon?"

"A short one," Clay affirmed. "My hands arranged an overnight at the Elms in Denver."

Clay cleared his throat and Gaby noticed his cheeks had flushed. It seemed the playacting never got easier.

"I suppose one night's better than nothing," Sam said. "But you kids ought to really celebrate. After all, a wedding is a life-changing event."

"Maybe later. When things slow down around here."

Clay made the comment so casually Gaby almost believed it herself. But there would be no "later."

As they continued eating, Gaby grew more and more anxious. Her stomach felt so queasy she could scarcely swallow.

"Gabriella, may I ask you a favor?"

"Certainly, Mrs. Forrester."

Clay's mother folded her napkin and laid it on the

table. "Mrs. Forrester sounds terribly formal. I was wondering if . . ." She hesitated. "Oh, never mind. I'm rushing things."

"Would you prefer I call you Barbara?" Gaby volunteered.

"Frankly, I wish you'd call us Mom and Dad."

While the request startled Gaby, the hope in Barbara's eyes made it hard for her to refuse. She glanced at Clay's father, whose eyes reflected the same hope. "I'd be pleased to call you Mom and Dad," she said, unable to take away that hope.

Barbara's smile was radiant. "Oh, thank you, Gaby. It means so much, doesn't it, Sam?"

Clay's father literally beamed. "You bet it does."

They finished supper and Gaby started clearing the table but Barbara stopped her. "You kids go read the newspaper. Dad and I will do dishes."

So Gaby and Clay retired to the living room where they read the paper together as they'd done for several evenings now. A short time later, Clay laid the paper aside and studied Gaby intently.

She squirmed under his gaze. "What?"

"Nothing."

But he continued studying her, which caused Gaby's cheeks to flush and a warm glow to spread through her body. "What is it, Clay?"

"Thanks for indulging my mother. I know how close you were to your own mother. That was no small request."

"Your mom's a sweet lady," Gaby assured. "It won't be difficult at all."

A short time later, his parents joined them in the living room. They asked more questions about the wedding and their plans for the future. Gaby sighed. She could barely handle the present.

Finally, Barbara and Sam retired to the guest bedroom while Gaby and Clay retreated to his room across the hall. As he closed the door, Gaby flopped down on the bed and covered her face with her hands. "I never dreamed this would be so complicated."

"You did very well," Clay soothed. "You answered every question believably."

"Great. That means I've become a pathological liar."

She lifted her head to gaze at him. Unfortunately, he'd just pulled off his shirt and she was favored with an up-close-and-personal view of his chest. She looked away but noticed her palms grew sweaty and a lump formed in her throat. Dealing with arousal and guilt at the same time might push her over the edge.

"Oh, Clay," she wailed. "Your parents are wonderful people. I hate fooling them this way."

"If you don't keep your voice down, Mom and Dad will hear you. Heck, the guys in the bunkhouse will hear you."

He sat down on the bed. The chest she'd tried so hard to ignore was right before her eyes now. Clay's nearness and tantalizing aftershave set her heart pounding.

Exhaling slowly, she said, "I'm in over my head. Way over my head."

"You're not in over your head."

She nodded vigorously. "Yes I am."

"You're doing fine, Gaby. Why won't you believe me?"

His voice was deep and husky and he was dangerously close. He smoothed her hair and his gentle touch released a host of feelings. Feelings she'd tried hard to keep tucked away. "Clay, I . . ."

"Ssssh," he whispered. "You're just tired. After a good night's sleep everything will look brighter. Remember, we aren't doing anything wicked here."

It seemed pretty wicked to her to be just inches away from this stripped-to-the-waist hunk of cowboy and pretend to be his wife.

"Did you see the way Dad's eyes sparkled when I told him we were married?"

Gaby nodded.

"He looked healthier. Didn't you see him come to life before your eyes?"

She nodded again. "So you don't think what we're doing is awful?"

"No, I don't. Didn't you do some things to make your mother happy during her illness?"

"Sure. I rented videos and checked out library books by her favorite authors. I even bought books on tape when she was too weak to read anymore. And I baked lots of chocolate cream pies. Mama hadn't let herself indulge while she was healthy for fear of gaining weight."

"See? You did the same thing."

Gaby raised her head and looked directly into Clay's eyes. Into those dark, sexy eyes. Oh, dear. That was a mistake. Hurriedly glancing out the window at the mountains, she tried to sidetrack her runaway emotions and let her brain take charge.

"Surely you don't place hiring a wife in the same category as baking pies and renting videos?"

"The principle's the same. Didn't the videos lift your mother's spirits and make her last days happier?"

"Well, yes."

"I rest my case."

He reached out and caressed her cheek and the tender gesture caused her to catch her breath. "Feeling better?"

"Um-hum," she lied.

"And tomorrow we'll go on just as before? Without you worrying so much?"

"Um-hum," she lied again.

"Good girl."

Instead of getting up as Gaby'd expected, Clay studied her a moment longer, then bent and placed a soft kiss on her cheek. "That's better," he said. "I don't know why you're upset when things are going so well."

Gaby was too shocked to reply.

Clay stood and stretched. "We'd better get some sleep."

Gaby felt both relief and disappointment as Clay moved away. It was easy to lose herself in this make-believe world they'd created.

They proceeded with their evening ritual. When Clay went to shower, Gaby slipped into her gown and made up the couch-bed.

This was her night for the couch. She rubbed her lower back that hadn't fully recuperated from the torture of sleeping on it two nights ago. By the time Clay returned, she was settled and getting drowsy.

"Gabriella?" His deep voice cut into her consciousness.

"Mmmmmm?"

"I want you to know that I appreciate your being here."

"Good," she murmured. "I hope it helps your father."

"It already has. Thank you."

"You're welcome."

Clay flipped the switch and the night light provided hazy illumination. The room had only been quiet a few moments when a knock sounded on the bedroom door. "Clay? May I come in? I need to talk to you."

Gaby recognized Barbara's voice and froze.

"Just a second, Mom."

Clay bolted from his bed and rushed to the couch where Gaby lay immobilized. "Get up quick. My mother's at the door."

His command got her moving and she sprang up and helped him yank the sheets off the couch and stuff them behind it. He grabbed hold of Gaby's shoulder. "Go hop in my bed."

She climbed into Clay's bed, wondering how she'd ever gotten herself into this predicament.

Clay saw the panic in Gaby's eyes. When he opened the bedroom door, he realized his mother was troubled, too. "Come in, Mom," he said, wondering how he'd handle two upset women in one evening.

His mother stood in the hallway looking hesitant. "I hate to disturb you."

"You aren't. Come in."

She did and went to sit on the couch that only moments ago had served as Gaby's bed. "I'm worried about Dad," she said.

"Is he having chest pains again?" Clay asked, hoping his mother didn't have more bad news to share.

She shook her head. "It's his mental state that concerns me. Dad's been depressed for weeks and it's so unlike him. He's always been cheerful and easygoing."

"But he seems positive and upbeat since you've arrived."

"There has been improvement," she said, a slight smile curving her mouth.

"Watch and see, Mom. Being at the ranch will turn Dad back into his old cheerful self."

"You think so?"

"I'm sure of it."

"I don't want to be a burden to you kids. Newlyweds don't need a couple of mopey people hanging around."

Gaby went over and knelt at his mother's feet and took her hand. "Don't worry about a thing, Mom. Clay and I will do all we can to cheer you both up. You've been through a lot recently."

Barbara smiled. "Oh, honey, you're so sweet and thoughtful. It was a lucky day for the Forresters when Clay married you."

"I'm proud to be part of this family." Gaby smiled. A sweet smile that lit her entire face. It seemed to Clay that she became more beautiful with each passing moment.

"After a good night's rest, you'll feel better, Mom,"

Clay admonished, realizing he'd preached the same sermon to his pretend wife just moments ago.

"I feel better already."

"Anything else you want to discuss?" he asked, hoping there wasn't. The women in his life were going down like flies and he'd done all the bolstering he could manage for one evening.

"No, honey. Thanks for everything."

Clay escorted his mother to the door and watched her cross the hall to the guest bedroom. Then he turned back to Gaby, who'd moved back onto the couch, looking paler than ever. Once again, guilt was stamped all over her features.

"Brutus must have felt like this just before he stabbed Julius Caesar," Gaby murmured. "Jack Ruby must have felt like this before he shot Lee Harvey Oswald. And . . ."

"I get the analogy," he said, dropping down beside her. "You're being too hard on yourself. You played a key role in lifting both my parents' spirits today. You should feel proud, not guilty."

When she glanced at him, frustration welling in her gorgeous green eyes, his heart skipped wildly. Gaby stirred feelings in him that hadn't surfaced since Jill.

"Oh, Clay, you could sell oil to an Arab. You're twisting this runaway marriage into something wholesome when it isn't."

As she stared into his eyes, Gaby looked extremely wholesome. And pure. And lovely. And for a moment Clay wished that Miss Gabriella Gibson from Atlanta really was his wife.

He pushed the troubling thought aside. "You're taking this too seriously," he affirmed. When you act in a play, you don't become the character, do you?"

"Of course not."

"You simply play a role. That's what you're doing here, Gaby. Just playing a part."

He thought he saw a flash of pain in her eyes. She took a deep breath and expelled it slowly. "You're right. I'll be more objective. I promise."

"Good. Now you sleep in my bed and I'll take the couch. You've worked hard and deserve a decent night's rest."

Gaby didn't resist. She crawled into his bed and within moments her gorgeous, sun-bright hair spilled all over his pillowcase. She lay there, eyes closed, looking like the goddess Aphrodite in that gown that exposed her creamy shoulders.

Clay sighed. It was all he could do not to crawl in beside his pretend wife and kiss the living daylights out of her.

It became easier and easier to get caught up in this little charade. He'd have to take his own counsel. Remind himself daily they were just acting.

He flicked off the light, burying the room in darkness. Then he climbed into his miserable, broken-down couch, and tried to pretend that the most desirable woman on the planet wasn't an arm's length away, snuggled contentedly between his sheets.

Chapter Eight

"**I** can't believe we've been here three days already," Barbara declared as the four of them sat talking on the front porch. "I don't know when we've had so much fun."

Sam nodded. "I'll second that. Coming back to the ranch has made a new man out of me."

Gaby and Clay sat in the porch swing while his parents occupied lawn chairs. Clay's arm rested casually on the back of the swing and his fingers stroked Gaby's shoulder. His touch, which felt like the caress of a thousand tiny feathers, made concentration difficult.

When Clay momentarily stopped, Gaby inhaled deeply, unaware until that moment she'd been holding her breath.

"So you're feeling better, Dad?" Clay asked.

"Lots better. There's something about the mountains that makes a man glad to be alive."

"That's for sure." Clay resumed the casual stroking and his slightly callused fingers sent delightful shivers racing up Gaby's spine.

Barbara smiled at her husband. "I knew a visit to the ranch would make you feel better."

"Well, you were right. I feel great. Good enough to go horseback riding."

Barbara's smile vanished. "Now hold on, Sam Forrester. You barely get around in your wheelchair. Riding a horse is downright stupid."

In spite of Gaby's difficulty concentrating, she caught Barbara's last comment and agreed. Riding a horse was downright stupid.

"Stop fussing, Barb. I won't ride alone. Clay will tag along, won't you son? Or better yet, all four of us can take a ride."

"Now, Sam."

"You'll go, won't you, Gabriella?"

Only one word of Sam's last comment penetrated Gaby's foggy brain. Her name. It came at her like gunshot out of the blue, breaking the mesmerizing mood Clay created as he traced delicate circles on her skin.

"What did you say, Dad?" she questioned.

"I suggested that the four of us go riding. Surely my new daughter-in-law won't refuse?"

Gaby gazed into Sam's eyes that were the identical shade of slate gray as Clay's. They filled with a passion for life, making it hard for her to refuse. "Maybe a short ride wouldn't hurt."

Barbara sighed. "I suppose you're right. I worry too much. But that's because I love this man. And want him to be careful."

Sam leaned over and planted an enthusiastic kiss on his wife's cheek. "You know, riding a horse is a lot like using a wheelchair. I don't do any of the work."

Barbara shook her head. "Sam Forrester, you're impossible."

As Gaby watched Clay's parents interact, she realized how deeply they cared for each other. She hoped someday to have a similar relationship. If she married Clay, could they share this same kind of happiness?

She pushed that renegade thought aside, reminding herself—for the umpteenth time—that theirs was a fabricated marriage, nothing more.

Clay slipped his arm from around Gaby's shoulders and stood. "I promised my hands I'd help with the fence. But I've got time for a short ride."

The ride could never be short enough, Gaby thought as the foursome made their way to the barn. Clay pushed his father's wheelchair and she and Barbara walked ahead of the men.

"I guess I'm overly cautious," Barbara told Gaby. "But I can't bear the thought of losing Sam. When you love a man with every fiber of your being, you always try to protect him."

"I suppose you do."

"You know how I feel, Gaby. You love Clay in the same way that I love Sam."

The comment shocked the breath out of Gaby. "I . . . I do?"

"Of course, you do. I can tell by the way you look at him."

"But Clay and I have only been together a short time."

"Time doesn't matter. It's how you feel about each other that counts. I've always believed that two elements make a great marriage. Love and respect. And you and Clay share those feelings."

The knot in Gaby's throat kept her from replying. She must be playing her part well to so thoroughly convince Barbara. For a moment, she wished she and Clay had the kind of love that Barbara assumed they did.

Clay's mother sees what she wants to see. That thought made Gaby feel empty inside. She scolded herself for again getting caught up in the charade.

But it wasn't all playacting. The more time they spent together, the more her feelings for Clay intensified. She'd been drawn to him from the moment they met—from that first mind-numbing kiss. And each day it became harder to ignore the emotions that swirled through her body.

Remember, you're an actress, she reminded herself. *A good actress.* All she had to do was keep her feelings for Clay locked deep inside her, and refuse to give in to the powerful emotions he stirred. Only two things mattered: that Clay's parents believed their son was happily married, and that his father's health improved. Thankfully, both of these were happening.

Clay saddled the horses and while he and his mother assisted Sam onto a tall brown horse, Gaby walked over to Cinnamon. "Remember me?" she asked softly. "I'm the lady you ran off with the other day."

The horse snorted as if she remembered.

Gaby inched closer. "If you're planning to do that again, would you wait till some other time? Please don't embarrass me in front of my in-laws."

Cinnamon snorted again and tossed her mane but Gaby stood firm. Reaching out a shaky hand, she stroked the horse's sleek nose the way she'd seen Clay do. To her surprise, Cinnamon quieted. "That's better," Gaby affirmed. "Maybe you and I will be friends, after all."

"Ready to mount, babe?"

Clay's sensual voice cut straight to Gaby's heart. As she turned to face her cowboy husband, her pulse galloped like the hooves of a racehorse. Partly from her fear of riding, but mostly from being close to Clay.

"Don't be nervous, Gabriella," he said quietly. "I'm with you all the way."

"Thanks," she murmured. Swallowing hard, she wondered what would it be like to have a man with her all the way.

"Slide your left foot into the stirrup the way you did before." Clay laid a reassuring hand on Gaby's shoulder.

She took a deep breath, then followed his instructions. It went easier this time and soon she was safely settled on Cinnamon's back. She flashed Clay a bright smile. "How was that?"

He shoved back his Stetson. "Darn near perfect, babe. Darn near perfect."

Clay's approval warmed Gaby's heart. *But it shouldn't*, she reminded herself sternly.

During the years she'd starred in plays, she'd played some mighty tough roles. Roles that deeply challenged her. But no role came close to the challenges she confronted each day as Clay's pretend bride. This, she knew, was the biggest acting challenge of her career.

The sun beat down with a steady, reassuring warmth as the party of four rode past the barns and bunkhouse to the open countryside. As far as the eye could see, Black Angus cattle dotted the landscape, grazing contentedly.

Sometimes Clay could scarcely believe his own good fortune. All the land for miles around was his land. That gave him a deep sense of satisfaction. And having his parents back home added to his happiness.

In addition, Gaby was convincing his mom and dad that they were a couple. He let his folks ride on ahead while he dropped back to talk to her. "Is riding any easier the second time around?"

The confident smile she'd flashed when she'd swung into the saddle had long since vanished. "Maybe a little," she said.

But her demeanor proved otherwise. Perched rigidly on Cinnamon's back, Gaby's expression was one of controlled panic. She reminded him of a contemporary Joan of Arc riding bravely to her doom.

While Clay knew the demands he made on his pretend bride were steep, he couldn't deny that Gabriella Gibson had grit. She hadn't backed away from a single challenge he'd presented her with. And he admired that.

His father's voice drifted back on the warm summer

breeze. "Why are you two lagging behind? Don't tell me you can't keep up with a couple of senior citizens?"

"Leave the kids alone, Sam," his mother chided. "They're newlyweds, for Pete's sake. They don't want to hang around with us all the time."

"They don't?"

"Of course not. Don't you remember what it was like to be young and in love?"

His father chuckled. "Frankly, honey, all I remember is what it's like to be old and in love."

His parents talked quietly for a moment, then his dad said, "Mom and I want to ride out to the property line. We'll meet you kids at the house later."

Clay nodded. "Enjoy yourselves."

His folks rode off, leaving him alone with Gaby. "They're having a great time," he told the lovely woman who rode along beside him.

She smiled. "I'm glad things are working out. Do you realize how lucky you are to have two parents who so obviously adore each other?"

"Guess I take that for granted. It's always been a given."

He noticed that Gaby had relaxed her death grip on the saddle horn. "I like your folks a lot, Clay."

"Well, the feeling's mutual. They think you're terrific, too."

"You think so?"

"You bet."

Gaby flashed that glorious smile and Clay realized he thought Gaby was pretty terrific himself. Her natural beauty and sensual charm intoxicated him. He felt slightly drunk right now, just looking at her.

Jill had intoxicated him, too, he reminded himself. When he married Jill, he thought he'd found a woman to love forever. But she wanted more from life than what he and his way of life could offer.

Gaby wanted more, too. She wanted big city lights, the theater, things that were foreign to life on a cattle ranch.

"We're not far from the cabin," Clay said, forcing himself to focus on the ride instead of on Gaby. "My folks planned to retire in the cabin and lived there briefly. Then Mom got the idea of moving to Florida."

"I'd love to see it."

"Are you sure? It's a ten-minute ride at the rate we travel."

Gaby took a stabilizing breath. "I think I can manage ten minutes. Unless the Johnsons' dog shows up again."

"O.K., then. Let's go."

The horses' hooves hitting the earth set up a comfortable rhythm as he and Gaby rode along. The sunshine warmed their backs and danced in Gaby's golden hair. She seemed more relaxed now. Clay hoped Shiner wouldn't reappear and destroy her shaky confidence.

"The cabin's just ahead," he said when they reached the clearing.

"Where? I don't see it."

"You will. The house blends perfectly with the landscape. Dad designed it that way."

Moments later the cabin came into view. "Oh, Clay," Gaby declared. "It's magnificent."

"Isn't it?"

Clay had always loved the little cedar house perched at the foot of the mountains. After sliding off Ranger, he secured the reins to the hitching post and went to help Gaby down.

"I can do it myself," she insisted. So he took a step back and watched her do a shaky dismount. The white jeans made her waist look particularly small. Clay figured he could circle that waist with his hands and fought off a compelling urge to do so.

Strands of hair danced around Gaby's face and her cheeks had turned rosy with the exertion of the ride. "There," she said as her feet hit the ground. "I hope you're impressed."

"I certainly am." And it wasn't just with her dismount.

"I told you you'd get used to riding."

"I wonder why your parents went off," Gaby mused.

"To give us some time alone. After all, they think we're newlyweds."

As Clay stared into Gaby's mesmerizing eyes, he felt an overpowering urge to pull her into his arms. Why couldn't he control his emotions where this woman was concerned? Must he keep pushing the limits of their relationship?

Shelving his inappropriate thoughts, he said, "Want a tour?"

"I'd love one."

He led her up the flagstone path to the front door. When he opened it, the hinges creaked in protest. Acting on a crazy impulse, he swung Gaby into his arms.

She squealed in surprise. "What are you doing?"

"Remember what the bellman said? It's bad luck not to carry your bride over the threshold. Everything's worked so well for us, I don't want to jinx it now."

But having Gaby in his arms only made matters worse. Her delicate scent, which reminded him of a bouquet of wildflowers, mesmerized him. He swung her down, but kept his arm around her waist. Somehow he couldn't quite let go. When his gaze locked with hers, Gaby's lips parted as if she wanted to speak, but no sound came out.

Clay's throat felt parched. Swallowing hard, he tried to tear his eyes away from Gaby's lovely face but couldn't quite manage.

They stood deadlocked. Fortunately, she lowered her eyes and Clay felt both relief and disappointment. "I'll take you through the cabin now."

Tossing his Stetson onto a nearby table, he forced himself to move into the living room, breaking the magnetic field that had held them together.

Thoughts of Jill again kicked in. She'd loved the cabin, too. Sometimes she'd pack a picnic basket and they'd share an intimate lunch before Clay had to return to his duties. A stab of loneliness attacked him as he remembered how much Jill's leaving had hurt. If he wasn't careful, he'd fall in love with another woman who would soon be leaving. That realization cooled his passion a bit. At least, for the moment.

As Gaby joined Clay in the living room, her legs felt unsteady. The shock of Clay's strong arms wrapped around her and the wonder of being held against him left her weak and breathless.

Glancing around the room, she tried to focus her attention on the physical surroundings rather than her out-of-control emotions. "The cabin's great. I love the stone fireplace."

"Dad and I did the masonry work ourselves."

"You have all sorts of talents I don't know about," she said, keeping her voice light.

After a quick tour, they returned to the kitchen. "How about a cola?" Clay asked.

"Sounds good."

They took their drinks to the living room and Gaby sank onto a soft leather couch. "I can't believe your parents ever left this place. It's a perfect retirement home."

"That surprised me, too. When Dad first said they were moving to Florida, I thought he was kidding."

He dropped into the easy chair and crossed one denim-clad leg over the other. The navy and red plaid shirt he wore made him look like the perfect cowboy. Just looking at the man made Gaby's heart race.

"I miss having Mom and Dad around," he continued, unaware of his profound effect on her. "They had their privacy and I had mine, but we saw each other often."

"Maybe you can find some other use for the cabin."

"Probably not until I retire." He shot her the crooked grin she'd come to love. "And that's a long way off."

If Clay married again, he and his wife might retire in this cabin. That thought filled Gaby with sadness.

Why should thinking about Clay with another woman hurt so much? Brushing the unsettling thoughts aside, she reminded herself she was stewing about something far in the future. And none of her business, anyway.

She forced her thoughts back to the present. "When are your parents going home?"

"Day after tomorrow. Their flight leaves at ten o'clock in the morning." Clay's forehead creased with concern. "I scheduled your return flight for that same afternoon. I thought you'd be anxious to get home."

A lump rose in Gaby's throat and she suddenly felt lost. "That's fine," she affirmed. "Leaving the same day makes perfect sense."

But she wasn't sure she meant the words. What would it be like to return to Atlanta and the life she'd been content with before she met Clay? Could she go back to dating Brett, possibly becoming engaged to him, without constantly comparing him to her pretend husband?

Living as Clay's bride showed Gaby a whole different lifestyle. She'd learned firsthand what it was like to have a "real" husband. To be part of a loving family. She stepped into a dream world that left her feeling confused and uncertain.

But it's not my dream, she reminded herself. Her dream was the hustle and bustle of big-city life. The joy of teaching acting to kids and taking her classes to see the wonderful plays the big city had to offer. Her dream couldn't come true in Land's End, Colorado. And she couldn't abandon her dream because of a few days of playacting.

Gaby went to gaze out the picture window, turning her back to Clay so he wouldn't see her sadness.

He joined her at the window. "I don't want to rush you, babe. You're welcome to spend a week or two at the cabin after my folks leave. I can change your reservation if you like."

"No need. I'll be more than ready to head home the day after tomorrow," she said, ignoring her feelings of loss and loneliness.

They stared at the Rockies that lay majestically before them. Wispy lavender clouds drifted around the snow-capped peaks that jutted into a cornflower-blue sky. The intense beauty of the countryside tugged at Gaby's soul. She was beginning to understand the magical pull of this ranch cradled in such an incredible setting.

She sighed. "I'm going to miss the mountains. I don't have a view like this from my Atlanta apartment."

"I reckon you don't." He rested his hands lightly on her shoulders and Gaby's body tensed. She tried to ignore the powerful sensations that even his casual touch aroused.

"Do you consider our mission successful?" she asked, realizing the pretending was nearly over and almost wishing it wasn't.

He squeezed her shoulders. "More than successful. Dad's happier than he's been in months."

"That's good."

Clay slid his hands up and down her arms the way he had the night of the barn dance, flooding Gaby with excitement.

"Whatever happens to Dad, we've made this time pleasant for him."

"I'm glad. I couldn't be happier if he was my own father."

He squeezed her shoulders again and another thrill of

pleasure rippled through her body. While this rough Colorado cowboy wasn't the type of man she'd dreamed of all her life, Gaby realized that no man had ever made her feel the way Clay made her feel. His rugged good looks and kiss of greeting had nearly knocked her off her feet. And she'd never quite recovered.

While her original attraction to Clay had been powerful, her feelings for him had changed. Had deepened. Now it wasn't just his great looks and powerful masculinity that appealed to her. While his strong male presence still drew her like a bee to honey, she was also attracted by the person he was. A man of integrity who loved this ranch, his family, and nature.

Several seconds ticked passed in agonizing silence. Gaby didn't dare move for fear of encouraging Clay. Electricity sparked wildly between them and if she wasn't careful, she'd end up in his arms again.

When Clay lifted her hair and kissed the curve of her neck, Gaby grabbed the window ledge for support. The ecstasy swirling through her left her breathless and sent all rational thoughts scattering. She struggled to hang onto reason, knowing she must stop him. But if she moved, or even breathed, Clay might think she wanted him to kiss her, or hold her.

Of course she did. More than anything in the world she wanted to embrace this larger-than-life cowboy—to get lost in the wonder of his embrace. But she didn't dare.

"I wish you weren't leaving so soon," he affirmed. "Won't you consider staying a little while longer?"

"Thanks for the offer," she said quietly. "But I need to get back home."

He let her hair tumble back around her shoulders. "Sometimes I forget you have a life in Atlanta."

"Sometimes I forget, too."

Glancing at her watch, Gaby said, "Don't you need to help build that fence?"

She regretted the words the moment they escaped her lips because Clay moved away from her. "I've neglected the ranch lately. It'll take weeks to catch up on the work around here."

When he took a step back, Gaby felt it safe to turn around. "Then we'd better go."

He nodded. Together, they walked to the front door and Clay reached for his Stetson.

Outside, he watched her mount but didn't offer to help. Her panic around Cinnamon had diminished. Her feelings for the stately animal now lay somewhere between uncertainty and a cautious respect.

As they rode side by side, Gaby realized this might be the last time she'd go riding with her cowboy husband. Funny, that made her unbelievably sad. But not nearly so sad as the thought of leaving him and returning to her apartment.

Her acting assignment was nearly over. Soon the curtain would drop on this short adventure, she'd take a bow, then return to real life.

Her life. Not some pretend relationship with no chance of becoming real. Once she got home, everything would feel right again. And this short rendezvous with Clayborne Forrester would be just a memory.

Chapter Nine

Gaby donned her nightgown, chastising herself for her overreaction at the cabin this afternoon. Keeping her perspective where Clay Forrester was concerned became a tougher assignment each day.

She'd just dropped onto the edge of the bed and started brushing her hair when the door swung open and her cowboy husband strode in. He was barefoot and wore only a T-shirt and a pair of faded jeans. The woodsy fragrance that was part of him mingled with the aroma of fresh soap, and his hair, damp from a shower, looked black as coal. Gaby caught her breath. The man could be Mr. January in a male pin-up calendar!

She vowed to keep her attention on brushing and off Clay. Closing her eyes, she forced herself to concentrate by mentally counting brush strokes. *One, two, three, four, . . .*

"Randy offered to fix breakfast tomorrow morning," Clay said. "To give you a break."

"That's nice." *Five, six, seven . . .*

"The hands want to make things easier for you. They like you a lot."

"I'm glad." She kept her answers short, hoping Clay would go on to bed so she could get her emotions under control. *Eighty-eight, eighty-nine, ninety.*

No. That couldn't be right.

Gaby gave up trying to isolate herself and opened her eyes. If she'd been bound, blindfolded, and stashed under the bed, she'd still have sensed Clay's electrifying presence the moment he entered the room.

He stretched out on the couch, propping his bare feet on the arm and stuffing a pillow under his head. His flexed muscles made him look positively delectable.

"You must be awfully uncomfortable sleeping on that couch," Gaby observed. "You'll be relieved when I go home and you get your bed back."

He shot her a troubled glance. "I won't be relieved when you go home."

"You won't?"

"I like having you at the ranch. The hands think you're terrific, my parents love you, and I . . ." He gazed at her, his eyes gauging her response. ". . . I like you. A lot."

Silence hung heavy in the bedroom as Gaby picked up the pace of her brushing. *One thousand one, one thousand two.*

She gave up counting altogether.

Clay cleared his throat. "As you know, Gaby, I love

my work. I love every job I do at the Silver Saddle from herding cattle to cleaning out the barns. But . . ." He hesitated, then added, "But I've been happier here since you came than . . ."

Gaby held her breath, wondering what he'd say next.

". . . than I was with Jill."

"You can't mean that?" As Gaby stared at her counterfeit husband, she saw a touch of longing in his eyes—the same kind of longing that had taken up residence in her own body.

"Doggone it, Gabriella, I'm going to say what I think even if it makes you uncomfortable. First of all, ranching is my life. But . . ." He hesitated, then said, "I was never completely happy here until you came."

Where did that crazy thought come from, Clay wondered as he stared down at the woman who so rattled his senses. Gaby looked shocked by his declaration—but no more shocked than he felt.

Confusion welled up inside him. The time he and Gaby had spent at the cabin today almost convinced Clay that what sparked between them was genuine. Never in his life had he struggled so to distinguish fact from fiction.

He went to Gaby, took the hairbrush from her and pulled her to her feet. "It's hard to explain," he said, his voice husky. "You're different from any woman I've ever known."

"Different good or different bad?" Gaby asked, her voice a little unsteady.

"Different in a special way."

Gaby was so tantalizingly close that Clay couldn't resist the urge to kiss her. Leaning into her, he placed a gentle kiss on her lips.

She hesitated a moment, then kissed him back. Before he could stop himself, his fingers got all tangled up in the hair she'd so conscientiously brushed.

He pulled her close and the sensation of her body against his caused a dam to burst inside him. A dam that held back feelings he'd kept corralled for too long.

He'd expected Gaby to back off. She'd once reminded him that kissing wasn't part of her job description. Instead, she melted into him. Clay lost himself in the kiss, in the wonder of this woman who meant more to him with each passing day. As he explored her lips, a low moan escaped Gaby's throat.

As if in a dream, Clay heard a light tapping sound. Was it his heart pounding?

Ignoring the sound, he deepened the kiss, letting all his desires for Gaby have free rein.

The sound grew louder.

"Clay? It's Dad."

Gaby pulled away. "Uh, oh," she said. "I hope nothing's wrong."

Disappointment shot through Clay at his father's unfortunate timing. "Don't move, babe. Stay exactly where you are."

He opened the door a crack. "What is it, Dad?"

"We need to talk. Alone."

Clay raked a hand through his hair. "Sure thing. I'll meet you downstairs in a minute."

He glanced longingly at Gaby, who stood exactly

where he'd told her to stand. The gown she'd worn on their honeymoon looked even more enticing than it had at the Elms Hotel, and her tousled hair positively glistened. She looked more radiant than ever.

She walked toward him. "Go ahead, Clay. Your father needs you."

He grabbed a button-down shirt and slipped it on. Then he left the bedroom and headed downstairs.

Did he mean what he'd just told Gaby? That he was happier since she came to the Silver Saddle than he'd ever been? Or was his rational thinking being corralled by his emotions yet again?

Good thing his father knocked at the door. All his good sense seemed to have vanished as thoroughly as rustled cattle. He needed a reality check and his father had provided it.

But as he went downstairs, Gaby's delicate scent swirled around him, making him wish he was still in his bedroom with his pretend wife.

Gaby sat in the center of Clay's bed and felt positively stunned. What had she been thinking when she allowed Clay to kiss her again?

You weren't thinking. That's the problem. Gaby's shaky control over this situation grew weaker every day. Did she need to wear a placard around her neck stating "I am only an actress" to remind herself of her position in this family?

She shivered at the memory of Clay's mouth pressing on hers. The stubble of his beard had felt rough against her cheeks, and his clean, masculine scent still lingered in the room.

Clay's words pounded through her thoughts. He'd said she was different. Did that mean he cared about her?

He just cares for you because you're helping his family, an inner voice whispered. *Because you're making his parents happy.*

Those thoughts burst the romantic bubble and Gaby gave herself a mental shake. Once again, their pretend marriage had taken on a life of its own.

But she already had a life of her own. A perfectly good life in Atlanta with everything she ever wanted. Why oh why did this great-looking cowboy affect her so powerfully? Why did he put her whole world on tilt?

Pushing the pain of wanting Clay out of her thoughts, Gaby crawled into her bed—his bed, actually—and vowed to keep their "marriage" firmly in control.

A long time later, Gaby heard footsteps in the hall. The bedroom door opened and closed and once again Clay's scent and presence filled the room.

"Gaby? Are you awake?"

Because she couldn't face him again tonight, she pretended to be asleep.

"Gabriella?"

Moments later, she heard Clay walk over to the window. He raised the shade, letting moonlight stream through the windowpane. Was he upset? What had he and his father talked about?

She stole a glance at Clay as he stood with his back to her. His strong shoulders seemed powerful enough to carry the weight of the world.

Running a hand through his dark hair, he sighed. He had his share of problems with an ailing parent, problems she understood only too well. She fought off a growing urge to go to him and slip her arm around his waist. But if she did, they'd end up kissing again, which would only make matters worse.

After several long moments, Clay pulled down the shade, darkening the room. Gaby heard the creaky springs rebel as he lay down on the couch. She sighed inwardly. The sooner the pretending stopped the better. For both their sakes. Clay's parents would leave the day after tomorrow. Gaby swallowed hard. And so would she. Then she and Clay could get on with their lives.

But could she return to Atlanta, leaving this cowboy and the Silver Saddle Ranch far behind? Could she pretend their "marriage" never happened? Or that the runaway attraction she had to her make-believe husband— that had become much more—didn't exist?

When Gaby awoke, she found Clay propped up on one elbow, studying her. She blinked several times to make certain she wasn't dreaming.

She wasn't. He lay on the couch, big as life and twice as handsome.

"Hi, there." His morning voice rumbled deeper than ever.

"Hi, back," she murmured.

His gray eyes looked sleepy, and his dark beard cried out for a razor. She wanted to reach out and let the prickly whiskers tickle her fingers.

"What did your father want?" she asked.

"He was having chest pains again," Clay said somberly.

"Uh, oh."

"I wanted to take him to the emergency room, but the pains subsided. He didn't want to worry Mom."

Gaby sat up and propped herself against the headboard of Clay's bed. "Your father's such a dear. How I wish he wasn't sick."

"Me, too. But at least we're making this time happy for him."

She sighed. "I suppose that's worth something."

"We'd better head downstairs to breakfast. Randy gets huffy when people drag in late."

Clay got up, then reached for her hand and pulled her to her feet. As they stood close, the world again came to a screeching halt. Gaby thought he might take her into his arms again—almost wished he would. But he didn't.

Good thing. They'd have never made it to breakfast on time.

A short time later, they went downstairs and gathered around the table with Clay's folks and the ranch hands. Randy served a whopping meal of scrambled eggs, sliced ham, fried potatoes, and buttermilk biscuits. When the ranch hands' plates were finally empty, Zeb asked, "You still planning to move the cattle to the South pasture, boss?"

"Yeah. And we'd better get moving. I'll meet you fellas at the bunkhouse in five minutes."

"Since your folks are leaving soon, you may as well hang around and visit," Zeb said. "Jonas volunteered to ride in your place."

"That right, Jonas?"

"Sure thing, boss. We'll manage just fine."

"O.K., then. Thanks."

The kitchen was considerably calmer when the hands left. As Gaby retrieved the coffee pot to refill everyone's cups, she noticed Clay's parents seemed unusually quiet. Finally his mother said, "I know you weren't feeling well last night, Sam. I heard you get up several times."

Sam sipped his coffee. "Just the old ticker acting up a bit. No need to be alarmed."

"But you haven't had chest pains since we left Florida. At least that's what you told me."

"It's true. But the doc said I'd have occasional angina. Nothing to worry about." He patted his wife's hand but Barbara uncharacteristically snatched it away.

"Something's bothering you, Sam Forrester," she snapped. "I know you like a book, so don't deny it."

Sam glanced at his wife, then ran a hand through his thick silver hair.

Barbara crossed her arms. "I'm not leaving this table until you tell me what's wrong."

Sam sighed. "I guess you may as well know the truth. I'm not anxious to return to Florida."

Barbara looked shocked. "You're not?"

"No, I'm not."

Silence reigned for several moments, then Sam took his wife's hand. "I have a confession to make. I hate Florida. I hate the sand, the hot weather, and the fact that I can't see the mountains from our bedroom window. And I also detest golf and shuffle board." He sighed again. "It's a great life for some people, just not for me."

Barbara looked stunned and Gaby realized she was

witnessing a private moment. Feeling like an intruder, she arose. "I'll leave you three alone so you can talk."

Sam's gaze met hers. "Stay, honey. You're part of this family now. Just as much as Clay."

Sinking obediently into her chair, Gaby almost wished that were true.

"I know how much you love our new life, Barb," Sam continued. "You worked hard on the ranch all those years and you always dreamed of retiring to Florida."

"But I thought you wanted it, too."

"Don't worry about me. I'll adapt."

Tears pooled in Barbara's eyes. "Oh, Sam, you're a fool and a traitor. If I believed in divorce, I'd file for one this instant!"

Now it was Sam's turn to looked shocked. "Calm down, honey. I said I'd adapt. Give me a little more time."

Barbara lifted her mug, sipped the coffee, then slammed in down, sloshing the dark liquid onto the blue-and-white checked tablecloth. "Men!" she declared. "We've been married for forty years and I still can't trust you! Why didn't you tell me you hate Florida? Why did you let me think you were happy there? You probably had an unnecessary heart attack because of the stress of living a lie."

Sam shrugged and opened his mouth to speak but Barbara stopped him. "Just shut up, Sam. How could you think I'd want to live any place where you weren't happy? Don't you know me better than that?"

"Gosh, honey, I . . ."

"If you'd been honest with me, we could have moved back to Colorado months ago."

Moved back to Colorado? The words struck Gaby like a bolt of runaway lightening. She shot Clay a panicked glance which he promptly returned.

"You mean you'd consider moving back?" Sam's voice was edged with anticipation.

"Of course, you silly man. I'd move back in a flash."

Gaby again glanced at Clay. The color had drained from his face and panic edged his features.

Sam, on the other hand, looked like the cat who'd swallowed the canary. "Whoooweee. You mean I can ride a horse again? Instead of that stupid golf cart?"

A grin inched across Barbara's face. "Of course, darling. You should have told me sooner. Promise you'll never again pretend to be happy."

Sam planted a kiss on his wife's receptive lips. "I promise, baby. Oh boy, do I promise."

Gaby kept waiting for Clay to break into the conversation and encourage his parents not to make another hasty decision that might backfire. Surely, he realized what such a move would do to their pretend marriage!

"Son, what do you think of all this?" Sam asked.

Clay cleared his throat as a bead of perspiration trickled down his forehead. "I haven't had time to consider it. But where you live is up to you and Mom."

Gaby kicked Clay soundly under the table and he jumped at the contact. She shot him another frantic glance.

Sam leaned closer. "Would you and Gaby object to our moving back into the cabin, son?"

Clay's eyes widened in surprise. He opened his mouth to reply but Barbara broke in. "We can't move back into the cabin. The kids need their space. They don't want their parents living practically next door."

As he realized his folks were serious about moving back to the ranch, Clay's heart plummeted. Everything he and Gaby worked so diligently to achieve was slipping away like soil eroding from a hillside.

But he couldn't bring himself to refuse his parents. If they wanted to move back into the cabin, he wouldn't stand in their way.

"Gaby and I would be pleased to have you move back." He glanced at Gaby, who looked pale and more vulnerable than she'd ever looked. He could see the foundation of their pretend marriage crumble right before his eyes.

"But this is an important decision," he continued, wanting his parents to give it sufficient thought. "Maybe you should discuss it a while longer."

"If you and Gaby have no objections to our moving back, there's no need for further discussion," his mother said firmly. "Now that I know what's bothering your father, and how to fix it, I don't intend to waste a moment's time."

So much for that argument. Both his parents seemed delighted with their hasty choice.

"And we won't pester you kids. We'll stay out of your way."

"That never was a problem, Mom. You know that."

His mother smiled. "I really have missed you, Clayborne. It'll be so good to come home. Especially with a

new daughter-in-law in the family. I think I'm more excited about moving back than your father."

Clay glanced at Gaby who looked even more shell-
shocked than on the night of their shivaree. He felt like
gathering her into his arms and promising her that everything would be all right. But how could he? All the rules
to the game they'd invented had suddenly changed.

In all their days of pretending, Gaby'd never seemed
quite so stricken. He was afraid she might buckle under
the strain. All this pressure could push her into a confession.

Hopefully not. His father's heart might not tolerate the
strain.

When his dad brought his fist down on the table, Gaby
jumped. "Then it's settled. Mom and I will fly back to
Florida, pack our things, and . . ." He hesitated, then
added with emotion, ". . . and come home. Where we
belong."

Once again, tears pooled in Barbara's eyes. Happy
tears this time. "Let's go riding, Sam. We've got a lot
to talk about."

"And a lot to live for," his father added.

Clay watched them go. Then he turned to Gaby, wondering what to say. Their pretend marriage had just come
to a screeching halt.

Chapter Ten

Just after his parents rode off, the telephone rang. By the time Clay finished his conversation, Gaby'd disappeared. He stepped outside and found her sitting on the back steps.

Jackson bounded toward her, then lapped affectionately at her cheek, which nearly knocked her off the porch. "We're done for, Jackson," he heard Gaby say. "Clay and I will be the next ones to confess."

Clay went to sit beside his make-believe bride. He knew they had to talk this out, but his thoughts jumbled together into one confused muddle. His neck felt stiff from the tension and he felt angry at the way the bottom had so quickly dropped out of their little scheme.

"I'm heading over to the Triple Q Ranch," he told Gaby. "Matt Quigley's decided to sell a really fine horse that I've had my eye on for some time."

"When are you going?" Gaby's bottom lip quivered slightly as she gazed up at him. She'd been completely unnerved by his parents' decision.

"Right away. I've waited weeks for Matt to decide to sell that horse. I want to get there before he changes his mind."

Gaby's skin looked pale as alabaster. And for the first time, her green eyes registered defeat. "It's over for us, isn't it, Clay?"

He felt his jaw tense. "Well, it doesn't look good."

"I thought we'd put your folks on the plane day after tomorrow and bring this exercise in holy matrimony to a close."

"Me, too." He shook his head. "Things were going so well. Too well, I suppose." He hesitated, then added, "Let's not tell Mom and Dad the truth quite yet."

"I hate to upset them. They're so excited about moving back." She sighed. "And so happy."

"Yeah, I know."

Gaby smelled like a field of summer daisies—fresh, and light, and sweet. Her golden hair shimmered in the morning sunshine.

Funny, she didn't seem like a stranger anymore. At this moment, she didn't seem like a well-paid actress either.

He sighed. His parents were getting a new start—another chance to live out their dreams. Clay's chance was slipping through his fingers. One way or another, Gaby would leave soon and he'd return to his life as a single man.

You live in different worlds, he reminded himself.

Gaby's a city girl and you're a rancher and always will be. But the thought of her leaving, while it was the only sensible solution, took a chunk out of Clay's heart.

When she turned to face him, his heart leaped in his chest like a horse spooked by a rattler. "You'd better get that horse before it's too late."

He stood. "I reckon so." Then he strode out to his Bronco without a backward glance.

Gaby watched Clay start up the truck and drive off, leaving a cloud of dust behind. She absentmindedly stroked Jackson's head, wondering how they'd ever write the next scene of this impromptu drama.

Could she and Clay possibly resolve this latest dilemma? She began mentally attacking the problem from all angles, finally deciding it was too big to solve without Clay's help.

Jackson spotted a rabbit and took off at a dead run, leaving Gaby alone with her thoughts. She'd better do something to occupy herself until Clay returned.

Maybe she'd bake a cake. A wickedly rich, loaded with fat grams, totally sinful cake. Chocolate, of course.

In the kitchen, she paged through a cookbook and selected a recipe called Triple Layer Fudge Ambrosia Torte with chocolate sauce. Chocolate, she knew from past experience, could elevate your brain chemistry. Right now, she'd try any therapy—Band-Aid or otherwise—to feel better.

After locating the necessary ingredients, she set to work. Half an hour later, she slid three round cake pans filled with batter into the oven. She'd just closed the oven door and licked a glob of batter from her finger when Clay strode in. Tossing his Stetson onto the kitchen table, he beamed at her as if he'd just won the lottery. "I bought myself one mighty fine little gelding."

"I thought you were going to buy a horse."

"A gelding, my dear Gabriella, is a horse. A male horse that's been castrated."

She felt her cheeks flush. "That's terrible. I hope they had a darn good reason for . . . for . . ." Unable to find a polite way to phrase what they'd done to the animal, she shut her mouth.

Clay shrugged his broad shoulders. "I hate to disillusion you, but castration's a common practice around here. And there are good reasons."

"Like what?"

He took a seat at the table. "You ask a lot of questions, city girl, but I'll try and explain. A horse that's been castrated is easier to train than a stallion. Gentler, too. A stallion, as I'm sure you know, still has his . . ." He stopped, cleared his throat, then added, ". . . his masculinity intact."

She sniffed. "I assumed as much."

"I want this horse for riding more than herding cattle. He's a beautiful roan with black spots." Clay's dark eyes sought hers. "He'd make a great horse for you, Gaby."

She tried to ignore what Clay's gaze did to her. With a single glance he called every nerve ending in her body to strict attention. "You mean he's mechanical?"

Clay's eyes sparked with humor. "No, he's not mechanical. Not hooked up to a Merry-go-round, either. He's a gentle, even-tempered animal. He'd make a great woman's horse."

"Well, you'll have to find some other woman to ride your gelding. This one's flying home tomorrow."

The spark that lit Clay's eyes dimmed noticeably. "Yeah. I almost forgot."

Gaby knew darn well they were discussing trivia because trying to solve their real problems was too painful. It was called denial.

She glanced at her pretend husband, who'd just propped one leg on the bench of the trestle table. "Want a cola?"

"Sure."

She filled two glasses with ice and soda and joined him. "What are we going to do about your parents?" she asked, bringing their lighthearted banter to a halt.

Clay shook his head. "I racked my brain on the drive over to the Triple Q. To be honest, I haven't a clue. My gut impulse is to keep pretending. At least for now."

"If you decide to tell them the truth, I'll help you."

"Considering Dad's weakened condition, I don't think that's a good idea. I'll tell them after they move back. There's no other way to handle this—unless . . ."

She brightened at the glimmer of hope in his eyes. "Unless what?"

"Unless we lengthen your assignment."

For a moment, Gaby felt a surge of wild hope. Was Clay about to propose? Did the man have marriage in mind?

"Why do you have to rush back home, anyway?"

"I suppose I don't," she said, surprised that considering a real marriage to Clay brought such excitement.

"You don't have any family in Atlanta who are waiting for you."

"That's true." Her heart beat as furiously as Jackson's tail when he'd bounded up to meet her.

"And you don't have to start teaching for several more weeks."

Gaby's heart plummeted as she realized Clay wasn't suggesting a real relationship. He only wanted to keep on pretending.

"I need to get home," she said quietly. "I have things to do."

He nodded. "Sorry, Gaby. I sometimes forget you have a life in Atlanta. What will you do with the rest of your summer?"

"Probably work in a friend's gift shop. Allison always needs extra help."

The oven timer buzzed, spurring Gaby to action. What a shame that she and Clay weren't more compatible. If they were, perhaps they could have built a solid marriage the way his parents had done.

Clay finished his cola. "I'd better help Jonas and the guys finish that fence."

After he left, Gaby felt worse than ever. For a few moments, hope sparked inside her as she and Clay discussed possibilities. But he wasn't serious, after all.

And why should he be? Their chance of a real relationship was non-existent. Clay hated the big city and she was a misfit at the Silver Saddle. Even if they loved each other madly, which of course they didn't, they'd never be able to create a lifestyle both of them enjoyed.

As Gaby removed the cakes from their pans, she noticed that two of the chocolate layers had risen nicely, but the third leaned heavily to the left. By the time she stacked it on top of the other two, she'd created a chocolate leaning tower of Pisa that even chocolate sauce couldn't salvage.

Just like our marriage, she thought dismally, which was about to come toppling down around them.

The remaining hours of Clay's parents' visit passed in a blur. Gaby played the role of wife and daughter-in-law to the hilt, figuring she'd be an Oscar contender if this were the real world.

Of course, it wasn't.

She and Clay had reached an unspoken agreement. They didn't discuss the complication of his parents' moving back to the ranch. Instead, they ignored it. More denial. She was turning into Cleopatra, Princess of Denial.

The morning of his parents' departure dawned rainy and gloomy. Gaby arose early and started quietly packing her things. Clay lay asleep on the couch, bent into an ungodly position that would make a chiropractor jump for joy.

She took a moment to study her sleeping husband. The sheet covered his lower body but his marvelous chest was again available for viewing. So were his muscled arms, golden brown from the hot Colorado sun. He moaned slightly, probably dreaming about how the fiasco of their pretend marriage would end. His lips parted slightly and Gaby felt an irrepressible urge to kiss him.

Clay was one handsome hunk of a cowboy. He'd

stormed his way into her life and her heart. As she studied him lying there so peacefully, Gaby suddenly realized that she loved Clayborne Forrester—loved him with her whole heart and soul.

The power of the emotion nearly consumed her. She glanced at Clay and let this marvelous realization run unchecked through her body.

But knowing she loved Clay only made this drama more complex. How could she endure the last hours of their charade knowing she'd fallen hopelessly, completely in love with her pretend husband? Tears filled her eyes and she grabbed a tissue to wipe them away.

Gaby managed to avoid seeing Clay until breakfast, which passed with its usual lively activity. When the hands left for morning chores, and Clay's parents went to finish packing, Gaby busied herself cleaning up the kitchen.

Clay pitched in and they worked together in silence. Finally he said, "I better see how the folks are coming." He left the room but returned a short time later. "Mom and Dad are almost ready. We'll leave in half an hour."

Suddenly Gaby couldn't bear the pretense any longer. It hung like an albatross around her neck. "Clay, this seems wrong. Very wrong. I think we should confess before your parents leave. Let's tell the truth and face the consequences."

Clay placed a finger over her lips. "Hush, Gaby. They'll hear you."

"I don't care. This pretending has to stop. I simply can't tell any more lies."

"I know how tough this is, babe. Come over here and sit down."

After letting the water out of the sink, Gaby dried her hands, then obediently followed Clay to the table. He smoothed a lock of hair out of her face. When he put his hands on her shoulders, his warm touch made her body tingle. "Things didn't work out the way we planned, did they?"

Clay's breath felt warm on her cheek. She wanted to lay her head on his shoulder and pretend this ridiculous drama never happened.

"I came here with one purpose," she said. "To earn enough money to pay Mama's medical bills. I never expected to . . ."

She stopped herself just before the words "fall in love" slipped past her traitorous lips. Taking a steadying breath, she glanced into Clay's slate-gray eyes, forcing herself to disguise her feelings. "I never expected to get so involved."

He reached for her hand and as his fingers circled hers, her heart lurched with feelings of love and desire. "Me, either. But it would be foolish to tell the truth now. I don't want to shock Dad just before he boards a plane."

Gaby sighed. "I suppose you're right." Forcing a smile, and forcing the acting to continue, she added, "I'll play the role of Mrs. Clay Forrester a little longer."

A touch of mischief danced in Clay's eyes. "Was pretending to be my wife really so awful?"

It's been wonderful, she thought. But she couldn't tell him how she really felt. "Pretending to be your wife has been nerve-wracking and full of surprises. But never awful."

"That's what I like. Rampant enthusiasm. Guess I'll have to settle for that less-than-glowing assessment of our marriage."

She didn't dare say more. Didn't dare tell Clay how thrilling it was to play the role of his bride. Or admit the terrible truth: that she'd fallen in love with him in the process.

As she assessed the great-looking man sitting beside her, Gaby knew she'd always remember Clay just like this: handsome, desirable, and in every aspect, an incredible man.

He winked at her and the gesture stirred up a surge of pleasure. "Look on the bright side, babe. We've accomplished a lot. You'll be able to pay off your mother's debts, and my parents . . . well, they're happy as a couple of lovesick adolescents. Or hadn't you noticed?"

Gaby couldn't suppress a smile. "It's hard to miss. I caught them kissing in the bathroom this morning. The door was open so I walked in and found them locked in a passionate embrace."

A devilish chuckle escaped Clay's lips. "That was typical when Amy and I were growing up. We finally learned to knock rather than barge into a room."

"I can't believe that a couple who have been married so long still enjoy each other so much."

"I guess that's what true love does for you."

True love, Gaby's conscience reminded. Not the fabricated kind.

Barbara called from the stairway. "We're all packed,

Clayborne. Would you mind bringing our bags downstairs? Dad insists on carrying them, but I think they're too heavy."

"Be right there, Mom."

Clay reached into his pocket and pulled out a piece of paper and handed it to Gaby. "I can never repay you for all you've done, but I hope this helps."

The gesture felt like a slap in the face. Gaby pulled away and shook her head. "I won't take your check. I care about your parents too much to accept money for helping them."

Clay's eyes narrowed slightly. "Now, listen to me, Gabriella. You will take this money and you will pay off your mother's debts. That was the agreement and I won't have it any other way." After tucking the check into her hands, he strode out of the room.

As Gaby glanced down, she couldn't believe her eyes. The check was made out for twice the amount they'd agreed upon. She could pay Mama's bills and bolster her depleted savings account, as well.

Tears filled her eyes. She ought to be thrilled. After all, earning this money had been her primary goal. But as the days passed, the money lost its importance. Now it wasn't what she wanted at all. What she wanted was Clay. And she was just about to lose him.

Hot tears splashed down Gaby's cheeks. Slipping a tissue from her pocket, she tried to compose herself. It wouldn't do for Clay's parents to find her crying.

After blowing her nose, she squared her shoulders. She couldn't quit now. She'd carry this charade through to the last curtain call if it killed her.

And it just might.

* * *

When Barbara and Sam were comfortably settled in the back seat of the Lincoln, they all set out for the airport. The senior Forresters chattered like a couple of newlyweds. They giggled and made plans for their future. This man, who'd almost died of a heart attack just weeks ago, seemed positively reborn.

The back-seat chatter lowered to an undertone and Gaby only caught a word here and there. Then she heard Sam say in a hoarse whisper, "Let's tell them now."

"Do you think we should?" Barb whispered.

"Absolutely."

Barb cleared her throat. "Kids, Dad and I are giving you a wedding present. We're throwing a reception for you next month at the Silverthorn Country Club."

Clay, who was passing a semi, nearly broadsided it instead. "You're what?"

"We're giving you a wedding reception," Barb continued. "We want to throw a really big bash. You know how folks around here love celebrations, Clayborne. Since you cheated them out of a wedding, a reception's just the thing."

Clay's knuckles whitened on the steering wheel and his forehead wrinkled in concern. He didn't look the least bit like a happy bridegroom.

Shooting her a horrified glance, he said, "Gaby and I don't want to make a fuss, Mom. That's why we eloped in the first place."

"Now don't argue, son. I've already reserved the Country Club for July Third."

"It's a very sweet gesture," Gaby said, as panic attacked her yet again. "We don't want to seem ungrateful, but. . . ."

"No buts about it, Gabriella," Sam affirmed. "We're dying to show off our new daughter-in-law. Surely you won't deny us that privilege?"

Gaby looked at Clay and shrugged.

"Then it's settled," Barbara said. "The Forrester wedding reception will be held Saturday, July the Third, at seven-thirty p.m."

Sam chuckled. "You sound like an engraved invitation."

"That's a great idea. We'll send invitations as soon as we get back to Florida. Now, Clayborne, you must admit that you're a teensy bit excited about this celebration."

Clay looked like he'd rather be pistol whipped than attend. Or dragged by a wild stallion. He'd taken the news of his parents moving back to Colorado better than the announcement of the wedding reception. "Give me time to get used to the idea," he mumbled.

"You know, son, this visit has changed my life," Sam said seriously. "After my heart attack, I thought I had nothing to live for. But spending time with you and Gaby made me reconsider. I don't know when I've been so happy."

"I second that," Barb confirmed.

Gaby realized that she and Clay had achieved their objective. They'd convinced his parents they were deeply in love. Why wasn't she pleased instead of heartbroken?

The chattering resumed in the back seat and Gaby glanced over at Clay, who stared straight ahead. His body was rigid and he held the steering wheel in a death grip.

Gaby could identify. But instead of feeling tense, she felt suddenly limp—as if the blood had been drained from her body and all her muscles had jumped ship.

How could their carefully made plans have gone so far afield? Each day brought more complications. Their pretend marriage had mushroomed into a man-eating plant that was consuming them both.

The men checked the bags while the women went to the snack shop for a cold drink. As Gaby sipped her cola, Barb said, "You know, I didn't expect to feel this happy again. After Sam's heart attack, I was so afraid of losing him."

Gaby nodded. "That's understandable."

"I'd never lived in fear before. Throughout our married life, I felt safe and happy. Some of our friends' marriages broke up, but I never had a single doubt about ours."

"It must have been reassuring to be so certain of your husband's love," Gaby said, wondering what that kind of confidence felt like.

"It was. But then Sam had his heart attack and everything changed. I've lived with so much fear lately I could barely function." She smiled and covered Gaby's hand with hers. "But then we came to the ranch where I've learned the most important lesson of my life."

Gaby leaned forward. "What's that?"

"That nothing in life is certain. Each day is a gift to be treasured. While I fervently hope Dad and I have lots of happy tomorrows, I'll accept whatever comes and be thankful. You see, Gaby, life holds no guarantees."

Gaby expelled her breath. "I admire your courage, Mom." She sipped her cola, then added, thoughtfully, "You aren't the only one with fears, you know. I worry a lot about . . ." She paused, uncertain how to proceed. "About marriages that don't last."

"Surely you're not worried about your own marriage? Why, Clayborne adores you, honey. It's written all over him."

That major news bulletin made Gaby's pulse pick up speed. "You think so?"

"I know so. I raised that husband of yours and can read him like a book. Clayborne loves you with all his heart."

For a moment, the glowing words warmed Gaby and gave her hope. Barbara patted her hand. "Clay would have never married you if he didn't."

The hope inside Gaby died like a rose out of water. Clay hadn't married her. The only marriage he'd offered was one with a termination date. He was her employer— a man who'd helped restabilize her financial life. The painful truth felt like an arrow in her heart.

Moments later, Clay and Sam came toward them. Just looking at Clay's proud stride and his easy confidence increased Gaby's heart rate.

"It's almost time. We'd better get over to our gate," Sam declared.

The party of four made their way to the boarding area. As Gaby hugged first Barbara and then Sam, her eyes misted with tears. "Good-bye, Mom and Dad," she said, meaning the words. These two loving people seemed like her real family.

When a tear slid down Gaby's cheek, Barbara brushed it aside. "No need for tears, honey. We'll be back before you have a chance to miss us." She leaned closer and whispered, "Now remember, Gaby, no more doubts about Clay. Promise?"

She forced a smile. "Promise."

As Sam and Barbara walked toward the jetway, Gaby turned to her pretend husband. "I'll never see them again, will I?" The awful certainty settled over her like a heavy fog.

Clay slid his arm around her waist and the feel of his strong body so close filled her with longing.

Hang on tight, Gaby told herself. She only had to play-act a few moments longer. She'd manage even if it broke her heart.

Barb waved just before she and Sam entered the jetway and Gaby and Clay waved back. Then the senior Forresters disappeared from sight.

"We did it." Clay pulled Gaby close and she let herself lean into his strength this one last time. She hoped Clay didn't notice the tears streaming down her cheeks.

Back at the house, Gaby stuffed her clothes into the suitcase. She wanted to get away from the Silver Saddle Ranch and put this traumatic nightmare behind her as soon as possible.

Clay appeared in the doorway. "How are you doing?"

Just the sight of him made Gaby's heart skip erratically. She gave her eyes license to roam over the tall, muscular frame of this man who'd come to mean the world to her. "Fine, thanks."

She'd lied again. But she probably wouldn't recognize the truth if it came up and bit her. She fought to force down the lid of her suitcase, but it refused to cooperate.

"Here, let me help." Clay strode toward her and his fresh, male scent flooded her senses. She wanted to memorize that scent—carry it with her always. Within seconds he'd snapped the suitcase shut.

"Thanks," she said numbly, knowing this would be the last time she and her pretend husband would be alone in his bedroom.

Now that the acting was over, would he forget all about her? Could he put their relationship glibly aside? Or did they have a relationship to put glibly aside?

There was a solemnity about Clay she hadn't observed before. He'd pulled away from her emotionally. Never had she sensed so much distance between them—like a chasm that couldn't possibly be crossed.

He sank onto the bed. "Sit down a minute, Gaby," he said gently.

She dropped onto the couch across from him but couldn't meet his gaze.

"I haven't told the hands you're leaving today. They'll be real disappointed."

Gaby wanted to say she'd miss them, too. That each of the men held a special place in her heart. But she didn't trust her voice. She wasn't a good enough actress to play this little drama to a big finish.

Clay rubbed his forehead. "I'd like to put off telling them the truth. But that's selfish as well as impossible."

His eyes that had so often sparked with life now looked dull and hardened. And his mischievous grin was noticeably absent.

Clay's position was worse than her own, Gaby realized. Once she left the ranch, her assignment ended. She had no more explaining to do. But Clay had lots of people to set straight.

Suddenly an idea flashed into her thoughts. "Maybe you could postpone telling them for a little while. I enrolled in a two-week course at Emory University that starts next week. You could tell the guys that I flew to Atlanta for a graduate class." An ironic grin teased her lips. "You'd actually be telling the truth for a change."

Hope washed over Clay's handsome face. "That might work. It would let me break the news more gently."

For some crazy reason, Gaby's suggestion brought Clay some comfort. The idea that she might just be gone for a short time—that she would return and they could continue their relationship—flashed a beam of light into the darkness that circled his heart.

Gaby's luscious green eyes were wide with concern, and Clay wanted more than anything to touch her. Just to hold her hand or stroke her cheek. Better yet, to pull her into his arms, kiss the living daylights out of her, and beg her not to go.

Of course he didn't. Gaby had a life waiting for her in Atlanta. Her life. He had no business asking her to stay.

Glancing at his watch, he said, "We'd better get to the airport or you'll miss your plane." The smile he forced hurt, and the lump in his throat nearly choked him.

As they both stood, their eyes caught and held. How could he let Gaby go? How could he possibly live without her?

She looked away first and reached for the handle of her suitcase, but he beat her to it. "All set?"

"All set." Her smile seemed as forced as his own.

The second trip to Denver International Airport contrasted dramatically with the first. There was no one in the back seat giggling and making plans for their future.

No one in the front seat, either.

After checking Gaby's luggage, they hurried to gate 27. Clay shifted awkwardly from one foot to the other, not knowing what to say. Everything he'd rehearsed seemed superficial. Or patronizing. But he had to say something.

"Thanks for everything, Gabriella," he finally mumbled. "I appreciate all you've done." While his mouth formed the words, his heart screamed, "Please don't go."

As he gazed at the woman that so rattled his senses, she flashed her captivating smile. The one that warmed his soul and made his palms sweat. "I should thank you. I'll never forget the time I spent at the Silver Saddle Ranch."

Her words seemed too casual and her smile too bright. Tears glistened in her sea-green eyes and threatened to spill down her cheeks, but didn't. They just wavered, ready to overflow.

Like his heart.

She shrugged. "Sorry about the new complications."

"Don't worry. I'll work it out."

A voice over the intercom called for Gaby's row to board. She reached for her carry-on but once again, Clay beat her to it. If he couldn't touch her, he had to touch something that belonged to her. One last time.

As Gaby walked toward the jetway, each step she took led her out of his world and back into her own. The feeling literally ripped him in two. When she turned to wave, Clay drank her in hungrily, realizing he would never again see this amazing woman who had completely captured his heart.

Then he turned and headed toward the parking lot and the lonely life that awaited him, wondering how he'd ever cope without Gaby beside him.

Chapter Eleven

Gaby gazed out the window of the airplane at the lightening streaking across the sky. By the time her plane touched down in Atlanta, the storm had intensified. But it couldn't compare to the storm she felt within.

By the time she reached her apartment house the rain finally subsided. She stepped into the hall, then unlocked her front door and entered the shelter of the place she'd called home for the past four years. It had always seemed cozy, but not today. She felt as if she'd entered a stranger's dwelling.

For security reasons, she'd closed the draperies before leaving town so the apartment was dark as well as musty. Setting down her bags, she hurried to open the drapes.

The view actually startled her. All she could see was the neat brick structure of the apartment house next door.

Funny, that never bothered her before she went to Colorado. It bothered her now.

The days she'd spent at the ranch with its spacious rooms and glorious view of the mountains had spoiled her. At the Silver Saddle Ranch, she'd felt in touch with nature in a way she never had before.

She gazed around her orderly living room. The picture hanging over her fireplace, a spectacular view of downtown Atlanta at night, had seemed perfect when she'd purchased it several months earlier. Now it seemed all wrong. Her entire life had changed since she'd made that purchase.

It'll take a while to readjust, she reminded herself.

After carrying her bags into the bedroom, she unpacked. Then she wandered into her small kitchen where everything looked neat and organized. But compared to the ranch kitchen, it seemed lifeless. No rough-edged cowboys would storm in here expecting her to serve up a man-sized meal.

She flipped on the radio in an effort to drown out the silence. But when a voice began crooning about a brokenhearted cowboy who'd lost his love, she snapped it off fast. While the words didn't apply to her situation—Clay wasn't brokenhearted and he didn't love her—the melancholy lyrics made her feel even worse.

Sitting down at her kitchen table, Gaby buried her face in her hands and let the dam of loneliness inside her burst. Tears streamed down her cheeks and sobs shook her body. She hadn't cried like this since Mama's death.

When the tears finally stopped, she dabbed at her eyes and blew her nose.

A thought suddenly struck her. It wasn't the ranch house she so desperately missed. Not even the breaktaking view of the mountains. Not the noisy ranch hands gathering around the breakfast table, either.

It was Clayborne Forrester, the drop-dead gorgeous cowboy who'd hired her to play the role of his wife. She'd played the part as well as she could. Too well, obviously. Because she didn't know how to stop.

When the alarm jerked Clay from a restless slumber, he groaned with pain. The couch had once again wreaked havoc on his spinal column.

But he was getting used to that. Sleeping on this man-eating couch was worth doing only because Gaby was close by. Glancing at his bed, he searched for her delectable form. Then the truth struck him with sickening intensity. Gaby had flown back to Atlanta yesterday afternoon.

Reality hit with the force of a hurricane. He hadn't been able to force himself to sleep in his bed last night. It seemed like Gaby's bed now. When he'd folded back the covers, the sheets still held her delicate scent, and he could almost picture her curled enticingly beneath his comforter. Attacked by a profound sense of loneliness, Clay had remade the bed and returned to the broken-down couch. Even on the couch, it took hours to fall asleep.

As his feet hit the floor, Clay also remembered that he had to replace Gaby as breakfast cook. He pulled on jeans and a T-shirt and hurried downstairs, dreading what lay ahead. He'd have to tell his foreman and his hands that his "wife" was gone.

Minutes later, the bacon sizzled in the skillet and coffee gurgled into the pot. Should he hit his men with the truth and get it over with? Or prolong the agony by mentioning the graduate course?

The back door opened, then banged shut and Randy barged in wearing his contagious smile. "Mornin', boss. Where's Miz Gabriella? Don't tell me you let her sleep in for a change?"

The question increased Clay's sense of loss. He didn't know if Gaby was sleeping in or not. He didn't even know what her apartment looked like. All he had was her address. At least he'd had sense enough to have her write it down before she left.

"I'll fill you in when the others get here," he mumbled.

Randy shrugged. "Whatever you say."

The rest of his hands gathered around the table and after the food had been passed, Clay cleared his throat. "I have some news." He cleared it again hardly able to speak. "About Gaby."

Zeb, who was ready to shove a forkful of scrambled eggs into his mouth, set it back on his plate instead. And Randy stopped his coffee mug mid-air. "What about Miz Gabriella? She's all right, isn't she?"

Clay's mind flip-flopped between giving them the facts and holding out some hope, even if it was false hope. Still unable to decide, he said, "Gaby went back to Atlanta."

Randy slammed his mug down hard. "Back to Atlanta? What on earth for?"

The moment of truth had arrived and Clay couldn't face it. If he admitted to his men that his relationship with Gaby was just pretend, he'd have to admit it to himself. And he couldn't manage that.

"She's . . . um . . . taking a graduate course at Emory University. It's an intensive two-week session that's only offered once a year." He'd made up the once-a-year part to make Gaby's leaving seem more credible.

Seems he'd turned into a master prevaricator. Frankly, he didn't like himself much.

Randy wiped his forehead with the back of his hand. "Whew! I thought something went wrong between you and Miz Gaby. You scared me spitless."

"I suppose we can manage without her for two weeks," Zeb observed. "But it'll be tough. You're nowhere near as good-looking as your wife," he said, grinning.

Conversation turned to ranch-related subjects and Clay listened, answering only direct questions. He forced down some eggs but couldn't stomach the bacon. Gaby had finally mastered the art of frying bacon. And hers never tasted this greasy.

Suddenly, he remembered why. She'd laid out the strips on paper towels like rows of disciplined soldiers. Then she covered them with another layer of towels. He'd teased her about the practice but she'd kept right on. "If you have to eat meat, at least soak off as much grease as possible."

A tug of sadness pulled at Clay's heart as he recalled

Gaby's vegetarian preferences. If she were still here, he'd fix her a huge vegetarian omelet for lunch.

But she wasn't here. She was gone.

"With Miz Gaby away for two weeks, you're gonna be one lonesome cowboy," Randy observed.

The comment was just man-talk and not meant to insult, but it riled Clay all the same. Randy assumed he and Gaby lived together in connubial bliss. He almost burst out laughing at the irony.

"With all the work we have to catch up on around here, I'll hardly know she's gone," Clay snapped.

Then he sighed inwardly. Another earth-shattering lie had just escaped his lips.

The following week passed in a fog. Clay threw himself into his work, trying to forget the pain of losing Gaby.

One afternoon, he saddled Ranger and took a long ride. He had to escape the ranch house where memories of Gaby filled every corner. He rode to the cabin and spent some time in the small house his parents would soon reclaim.

That didn't help, either. He vividly recalled carrying Gaby over this very threshold. Of standing at the living room window with his arms wrapped around her. How he'd delighted in the feel of her sweetly-scented body molding so perfectly to his own.

As he looked at the fabulous mountains, a shocking realization struck him. He loved Gabriella Gibson! He didn't just miss the woman because of her great looks.

Or because he'd gotten used to having her at the ranch. He loved Gaby. Absolutely, positively loved her.

The realization sobered him fast. He'd loved Jill, too, and their relationship had ended in disaster.

He rode home slowly and had just put Ranger in the barn when Jonas bounded out the kitchen door waving a letter. "Why didn't you tell me about the celebration?"

"What celebration?"

Jonas started to read. "Mr. and Mrs. Samuel Forrester request the honor of your presence at a wedding reception in honor of their son and daughter-in-law . . ."

"Oh, that celebration." Clay cut his foreman off, unable to listen to any more.

"Yup, that one. It's not like you have a wedding reception every day."

The deep, dark secret, with its host of accompanying problems, suddenly erupted inside Clay. He couldn't live with it a moment longer. "Jonas, can I talk to you? Confidentially?"

Jonas nodded. "You bet."

They walked over to the corral where Clay rested his forearms atop the railing and gazed numbly at his horses prancing playfully inside. He finally made himself put the awful truth into words. "Gaby's not coming back."

"Not for another week," Jonas amended.

Clay turned to face his foreman. "She's never coming back. She's gone for good."

A flash of pain crossed Jonas' face. "But what went wrong? You two seemed a perfect match."

Clay gazed back at the horses and suddenly the whole insane story came spilling out. He vented his agony into the June afternoon with only Jonas and a few strutting horses as listeners. When he'd spewed out all the ridiculous, convoluted facts, Jonas digested them carefully before speaking. Finally, he asked, "Do you love her?"

Clay's eyes met those of his foreman and trusted friend. "With all my heart."

"Then don't make the same mistake you made with Jill."

The words hit Clay's gut hard. "Mistake? What mistake did I make with Jill?"

"When she left, you didn't go after her."

"Jill hated the ranch. I had to let her go."

"But she loved you, boss. If you'd gone after her, Jill might have come back. And with a little more time, she might have adjusted to ranch life."

The revelation hit Clay with powerful intensity. Had he been wrong? Could he have saved his marriage?

He pondered that possibility for several painful moments, then said, "You may be right about Jill. But Gaby's different. She loves Atlanta and big-city life. Living on a ranch would be like moving to a foreign country. She told me so a thousand times."

Jonas grinned. "Probably because she was falling in love with you. And was just plain scared."

If only he could believe that. "You honestly think Gaby loves me?"

His foreman chuckled. "You'd have to be plum stupid not to notice. No offense, boss."

Clay's thoughts suddenly swirled with new possibilities. Did his pretend wife love him? Should he go after her?

"But Gaby has her own life in Atlanta," he retorted, afraid to hope, afraid to be hurt again. "And a teaching career."

"Last I heard, there were some darn good high schools in the Denver area. And all of them hire drama teachers."

A faint silver lining edged the dark cloud that had engulfed Clay since the moment Gaby walked out of his life. He grinned at Jonas. "So you think I should go after her?"

"Absolutely."

"Gosh, I missed you, Gabriella. What were you doing in Colorado all that time?"

Brett Logan stared at Gaby across the table of The Garden Tea Room where they'd come after seeing a production of *The Taming of the Shrew*.

Unable to meet his eyes, Gaby took a bite of her strawberry torte. "I visited a friend who lives on a ranch. The Silver Saddle Ranch."

Brett laughed out loud. "It's hard to picture you on a ranch, Gabriella. How on earth did you spend your time?"

Gaby shrugged. "I fixed breakfast for the ranch hands, learned to ride a horse, and . . ."

. . . *fell in love with a cowboy*. She stopped herself before that painful realization slipped out.

"You learned to ride a horse? Without falling off?"

"Believe it or not, I did."

When Brett reached for her hand, she didn't feel anything. No runaway thrill. No tingling. No nothing.

"I'll bet you missed the theater, stuck out there in no man's land."

"Not really," she said, realizing now she'd never once thought about the theater. And hardly ever thought about Brett Logan, either.

"I had too much to do to miss Atlanta."

"Well, don't go flying off like that again. I missed you terribly while you were gone."

"That's sweet," Gaby murmured, unable to tell Brett she'd missed him, too, because she hadn't.

"I bought you a little homecoming present."

Brett reached into the breast pocket of his expensive designer suit and pulled out a box. A ring box.

Gaby's heart lodged in her throat. "Brett, I . . ."

He opened the box which contained a sparkling emerald. "Now don't panic. It's not an engagement ring. It's a pre-engagement ring. Maybe by Christmas . . ."

Gaby slipped her hand out of Brett's as a sense of being smothered overwhelmed her. "I'm sorry, Brett, but I can't accept the ring. I simply can't."

A hurt expression covered Brett's handsome face and his blue eyes questioned. "Why not? I thought we were building a relationship here."

She reached back over and squeezed his hand. "We were, Brett, but something happened to change that."

He sighed heavily. "I feel I deserve an explanation."

Gaby took a steadying breath. "Well, you're never going to believe this because I scarcely believe it myself. But when I visited that ranch in Colorado, I fell head over heels in love with the owner of the Silver Saddle. And my heart belongs to him."

Brett ran a hand through his hair. "Of all the unexpected plot twists, this one takes the prize."

He was quiet for several moments, then asked, "Does this cowboy love you, too?"

"No."

It was all Gaby could do to squeak out the word. Admitting the painful truth tore a huge hole in her heart.

Brett slipped the ring box back into his pocket. "Then I refuse to give up. I'll keep trying to get you back, Gaby. You and I belong together. We want the same things out of life."

Gaby forced a smile. Brett's statement used to be true, but it wasn't true anymore. All she wanted out of life was one drop-dead gorgeous cowboy who'd stolen her heart.

After Brett brought her home, Gaby settled on the couch, turned on some quiet music, and thought about the disaster her life had become.

Each day she struggled to focus on the graduate class she'd paid top dollar to take—instead of the wonderful man she'd loved and lost. And all she did after she got home was review every moment she'd spent with Clayborne Forrester at the Silver Saddle Ranch—especially those romantic moments at the barn dance, in his bedroom, and at his folks' retirement cabin.

Her favorite memory was their first kiss, which occurred about thirty seconds after she met her rancher-husband for the very first time. As she recalled the incredible memory of Clay's mouth covering hers, she missed her pretend husband more than ever.

What had Clay told his hands about her leaving? How had he broken the news to his parents so they wouldn't mail out invitations to the wedding reception?

She sighed, realizing she must have played her part well to have so completely convinced Clay's parents they were a couple. When she'd expressed her fears to Barbara, she'd been shocked by his mother's reply. "Why, Clayborne adores you, honey. It's written all over him."

If only that were true. How different life would be if only . . .

The world was full of people who said, "If only . . ." Gaby determined not to be one of them.

Giving herself a mental shake, she went to take a shower, hoping to drown thoughts of Clay that had again consumed her. When she finished, she blew her hair dry and slipped into her nightgown—the same peach satin gown she'd worn on all those nights with Clay.

She turned down her bed and crawled between the sheets, remembering all the times she'd slept in her rancher-husband's bed. That seemed a lifetime ago.

She'd just drifted into the drugged sleep of exhaustion when the doorbell rang. Pushing herself to a sitting position, she rubbed her eyes and glanced at the clock. Who would come calling at midnight?

Picking up her cordless so she could dial 911 if need be, she tiptoed to the door. Peering through the peephole, she saw what looked like a miniature cowboy standing in the hall—one you might find in a Cracker Jack box.

Gaby's heart lodged in her throat. She tried to mentally inflate the tiny image to 6 feet 2 inches. Could that cowboy possibly be Clay?

Of course not. Clay was in Colorado. A whole world away.

Maybe she was asleep and this was just a dream. But the doorbell rang again and she jumped. Another glance through the peephole assured her this was not a dream. The cowboy standing on her front step could only be one cowboy.

Her cowboy.

She tossed the phone across the room and flung open the door. "Clayborne Forrester!" The name that burst out of her held desire, wonder, surprise, and every other joyous emotion she'd ever experienced.

Clay stood before her in all his masculine glory. He wore a tan shirt and a fringed leather vest that showed off his incredible shoulders. Jeans clung to his muscular legs and his scuffed boots looked out of place in her apartment building. He twirled his Stetson in his hands and his sexy grin made her pulse pound.

"I know it's late for company, but my plane just landed. And I have something important to ask you."

Gaby's happiness faded and suspicion kicked in. "Why did you come here, Clay? To arrange another business deal?" She lifted her chin, eyeing him cautiously. "What role do you want me to play this time? Your Aunt Martha from Buffalo?"

The roguish grin she'd missed so much lit his handsome features. Gaby tried to ignore what just looking at this cowboy did to her heart.

"What I want to discuss doesn't involve playacting.

May I come in? Or are you going to make me ask you in the hall?"

"Oh, um, sure." She flipped on the living-room light and Clay entered her apartment. His eyes quickly surveyed the room with its contemporary paintings and furnishings.

Then his scrutinous gaze took her in from head to toe, sending delicious shivers down her spine. "Won't you, um, sit down?" she stammered, trying to keep her cool while her heart raced wildly.

Gaby suddenly remembered she wore only her revealing nightgown. "Let me grab my robe," she said, turning toward the bedroom. "I won't have to borrow yours this time."

Clay reached out and caught her arm. Heat radiated from where his fingers touched her and thrills of delight ran unchecked throughout her body.

"Please don't get a robe. You look . . ." He paused and his eyes filled with longing. "You look like you did on our honeymoon."

Feeling her cheeks flush, Gaby sank onto the couch. Not so much to honor his request, but because her legs wouldn't support her a moment longer. Her pretend husband dropped into a nearby chair and Gaby waited for the next bomb to drop.

All Clay could do was stare at Gabriella Gibson. The fancy words he'd rehearsed on the flight from Denver balled into a huge knot and lodged in his throat. Gaby's hair, brushed into strands of gleaming gold, hung loose around her shoulders. And the gown of peach satin molded to the body he'd longed for, dreamed about, ever since she'd boarded her return flight to Atlanta.

Try as he would, Clay couldn't make his lips and voice box coalesce to form actual words.

After several moments of awkward silence, Gaby asked, "Did you tell your ranch hands the truth?"

He cleared his throat and two words came out. "Just Jonas."

"Have you talked to your parents since they returned to Florida?"

"They called last night." He'd miraculously choked out four words this time.

Gaby's gorgeous sea-green eyes looked anxious. "I'll bet they were disappointed when you finally confessed. Did you tell them not to mail out the invitations?"

"They already had. Jonas got his."

He'd graduated to six words now and almost felt he could actually converse with this vision of loveliness he'd been fortunate enough to hire as his bride.

He'd missed Gabriella Gibson more than any red-blooded cowboy ought to miss a woman. At first he'd fought the powerful emotion, but it had finally subdued him. He'd been roped as securely as a steer at a rodeo.

Gaby sprang to her feet and started pacing, favoring him with a full-length view of her stunning body. He swallowed hard, telling himself he didn't have a right to grab this woman and kiss the living daylights out of her.

"What are we going to do?" she asked. "Think how embarrassed your parents will be if . . ."

Subduing his emotions, he sprang to his feet. "Forget

the reception, Gabriella. I came here to tell you something much more important."

She whirled to face him. "Your father's not worse, is he, Clay? Because if you plan to share more bad news, I don't think I can handle it. I've been a total wreck in class all week. My professor thinks I'm a moron and I'll probably flunk this class—maybe even get disbarred from teaching and . . ."

He couldn't suppress a chuckle. "They disbar lawyers, Gaby. Not teachers."

She shrugged helplessly. "The point is my stress levels are already out of sight and I . . ."

Clay came toward her and placed a finger over her lips. Those soft lips he'd been dreaming of night and day. "Hush, Gaby, and listen to me. I came here to tell you that I love you."

Her green eyes shot wide open at his declaration but he couldn't discern what she was feeling. Was it joy? Panic? Disgust? What?

Her lower lip trembled. "You . . . you love me?"

"Yes. I love you."

"Oh, my." She expelled a pent-up breath. "This certainly comes as a surprise."

Clay braced himself for the forthcoming rejection. Several seconds ticked painfully past as he waited while Gaby still stood speechless.

"I know I have no right to love you, Gaby. You want a very different life from the one I can offer. But I just had to tell you how I feel."

"I'm . . . I'm glad you did."

"Before I head back to Colorado, I want to ask one question. Do you love me? I have to know."

When she turned and gazed into his eyes, hope spread through him like an erupting volcano. "Yes, Clay," she said. "I love you with all my heart."

His heart pounded so hard he figured it might pop right out of his chest. "You do?"

"Yes, Clayborne. I do."

"Listen, Gaby, I don't know how good I'd be at living in the city, but I suppose I could try. The Silver Saddle wasn't nearly as exciting a place to me after you left."

Her smile was radiant. "You won't have to move to Atlanta, sweetheart."

A thousand-ton weight slipped off his chest. "I won't? You mean . . ."

"I mean I miss the ranch something awful. I miss Randy, and I miss Jonas; I even miss Cinnamon. But most of all, I miss you."

Unable to keep his hands off Gaby a second longer, he pulled her close. "Then will you marry me? For real this time?"

Before she could answer, Clay covered her mouth with his. Partly because he'd die if she refused him. And partly because he could no longer keep his longing under control.

As his lips claimed Gaby's, Clay's heart took off like a spooked horse. A honey-warm glow spread through his body that had felt lifeless since the moment she'd left. When the kiss reached an intensity he'd never before experienced, Gaby suddenly pulled back. "Stop, Clay. I have to ask you something."

He tried to slow his pounding pulse and keep the passion at bay. It was hard enough to stop kissing this woman, much less concentrate. "Go ahead. Ask."

"Are you proposing to me just to make everything turn out right? So you don't have to confess to anybody?"

"No, Gabriella. I'm not asking you to marry me to make our concocted story come true. I'm asking you because I love you and want you for my wife."

"That's good."

She expelled a deep breath and seemed satisfied with that explanation. He hoped so. He'd like to get back to serious kissing. But it wasn't to be.

"Oh, Clay, we've made such a mess of things," Gaby lamented. "We've lied to so many people."

He tangled his fingers in her silky hair, finding it tough to hang onto a coherent thought. "I know, baby. I feel bad about that, too."

"We've just got to set things right before we get married. Tell people the truth. Especially your parents."

He could scarcely pull himself out of the throes of passion. "I already told them. On the phone last night."

She gazed at him in disbelief. "You told them our marriage was fake?"

"I did."

A surge of joy touched Gaby's heart as she absorbed Clay's words. If he wasn't proposing just to cover his tracks, he must love her.

Really love her.

"How did they take it?"

"Better than I expected."

While she wanted more than anything to kiss Clay, to

let this incredible kissing go on forever and ever, Gaby's head buzzed with questions. "How's your father?"

"The doctor said Dad's condition has improved. With proper diet, medication, and exercise, his prognosis is good."

"That's marvelous," Gaby exclaimed.

Clay's father was getting another chance at life. Gaby remembered Barbara's wish for more good days with her husband. It looked like she'd get her wish.

"Were your parents upset with us for deceiving them?"

"Not after I told them I was flying to Atlanta to propose to you. That cheered them up real fast."

When Clay bent to kiss her neck, Gaby shivered with delight. "You haven't given me an answer yet, Gabriella. Will you marry me?"

In that instant, all Gaby's worries flitted away. Not a trace of fear or hesitation colored this glorious moment. "Yes, darling, I'll marry you."

His slate-gray eyes lit with joy. "You've made me the happiest cowboy in the state of Colorado."

Questions began to flit through Gaby's brain. "Clay, how will we . . . I mean when will we . . ."

"We'll get married in Atlanta this weekend," he affirmed. "You can finish your graduate class while I head back to the ranch. The hands expect you home a week from tomorrow."

Gaby caught her breath at that awesome possibility. Stepping closer, she molded her body to his. "Home. That sounds great. But I have another idea. Why don't you spend this week in Atlanta and help me pack and close up the apartment. I'll go to class every afternoon and every night we'll celebrate with candlelight suppers. We'll get back to the ranch in plenty of time for our wedding reception."

Before Clay could reply, Gaby kissed him. Hard and long and with every ounce of the passion that consumed her. She pulled back just long enough to say, "Deal, Mr. Forrester?"

"Deal, Mrs. Forrester," he murmured, not taking his mouth from hers.